Books by Gilbert B. Cross

———————————

A HANGING AT TYBURN
MYSTERY AT LOON LAKE
TERROR TRAIN!

Terror Train!

Terror Train!

GILBERT B. CROSS

ALADDIN BOOKS

MACMILLAN PUBLISHING COMPANY   NEW YORK

MAXWELL MACMILLAN CANADA   TORONTO

MAXWELL MACMILLAN INTERNATIONAL
NEW YORK   OXFORD   SINGAPORE   SYDNEY

First Aladdin Books edition 1994
Copyright © 1987 by Gilbert B. Cross

Aladdin Books
Macmillan Publishing Company
866 Third Avenue
New York, NY 10022

Maxwell Macmillan Canada, Inc.
1200 Eglinton Avenue East
Suite 200
Don Mills, Ontario M3C 3N1

Macmillan Publishing Company is part of the Maxwell Communication
Group of Companies.

Printed in the United States of America
10 9 8 7 6 5 4 3 2 1

Library of Congress Cataloging-in-Publication Data

Cross, Gilbert B.
Terror train! / Gilbert B. Cross. — 1st Aladdin Books ed.
p.   cm.
Summary: Two boys, traveling from Chicago to Portland, Oregon, by
train, join forces with an elderly mystery writer to investigate a
fellow passenger's sudden death.
ISBN 0-689-71765-2
[1. Mystery and detective stories.   2. Railroads—Trains—
Fiction.]   I. Title.
PZ7.C88252Te   1994
[Fic]—dc20   93-25735

For the Characters
and G. P.
Who Made It Possible

Contents

Contents

Terror Train!

1

Rodney Gets Spots

"IT'S GERMAN MEASLES, ALL RIGHT," SAID DAD, PUTting the phone down. "The doctor's sure of it."

We were in our room in the Holiday Inn, Chicago. My brother Rodney, aged eight, lay in one of the big double beds with a thermometer sticking from his mouth. Our adopted brother, Vo Nguyen, stood in the bathroom door, a towel in his hand. He had on his red bathrobe with "U.S. Marines" written on the back in Japanese.

"Why didn't the doctor come out here," I said. "Maybe he should take a look at him."

Dad looked at me, shaking his head. "Jeff, doctors don't make house calls anymore. You wouldn't want them to leave their nice warm offices in weather like this, would you?"

That was a sample of Dad's sense of humor. Jeez! But it *was* pretty bad out. We had a ground floor room facing the parking lot, which was floodlit and piled up with snow. In the beam of the lights great white flakes fell silently, coating the streets with new snow and covering the old, which was piled up in dirty brown lumps along the curbs.

Rodney made a gulping sound; Dad ignored him. "The point is, lads, what do we do now?"

Nguyen toweled his straight black hair. I think he did it to stop laughing because this was typical Dad. He was forever coming up with a Plan, and something always went wrong. Always!

A week ago he'd suddenly decided that we should all go to Portland, Oregon, to spend Christmas with Mom. She plays first violin for the New Hampshire Symphony, and they always tour the West Coast during Christmas.

It had seemed like a great idea to Nguyen and me, and probably to Rodney, but Dad was never satisfied with the simple way of doing things. He wanted to fly to Chicago and then take the Amtrak train from there.

"Just think of it," he said. "Over two thousand miles by rail. We can get a bedroom because we'll have two nights on the train."

Then he went on about his old train set. He bought it about five years ago and called it a model railway. Dad spent hours building little houses and bridges for it. Trouble was it never worked; every time Dad switched on the juice, all the trains ran into each other or their lights went on, and they wouldn't move. Dad muttered about "blocks" and "overload" and all the lights upstairs would go out.

I was about seven at the time. Soon after, Dad started writing books and junked the train set so he could use the space for filing cabinets.

The point I'm trying to make is that Dad was forever getting excited about some deal, then changing his mind. Now we were stuck in a hotel room at nine o'clock, with a train to catch the next afternoon at two, and a brother with German measles.

Dad fastened the cord around his robe, pressing his glasses back on his nose. He brushed the hair across his bald spot in front and said, "I have an idea."

Nguyen stopped toweling, winked at me, and sat on the second bed. I took the easy chair by the lamp.

Rodney grunted several more times and waved an arm furiously. Dad stared at him in amazement, then remembered the thermometer and pulled it out.

"Gee, Dad," spluttered Rodney. "I couldn't breathe."

"Sorry, Rodders," Dad muttered. "The way I see it," he continued, vigorously shaking the thermometer, "is this. There's absolutely no sense in us all staying here." He glanced at me, then Nguyen. "Rodney will be fine, but he's got to stay in bed one more day."

5

"But, Dad—" I began.

"And," he continued, sitting next to Rodney, "Jeff, you and Nguyen can still go on the Empire Builder tomorrow; Rodney and I can hop a plane the day after tomorrow and meet you in Portland."

There was a knock. I padded across the carpet in my bare feet, looked through the peephole and began unlocking the door.

"It's room service," I said, opening up.

The waiter had a large tray piled up with food. Dad told him to put it on the table. Then, of course, he couldn't find his wallet to get a tip. His pants were in the wooden press we'd found under the mattress. Dad hadn't seen one of those in years so he had to try it. The waiter tried to pretend nothing unusual was happening as Dad dug under the mattress and wrestled with his pants.

By the time we were all settled down with plates of french fries, burgers, and cans of Coke, I'd thought it over. It seemed okay.

"Well," I started, "it—"

"Jeffy's scared to go on the train alone," said Rodney, in his most pesty way.

Ignoring him, I turned to Nguyen. He grinned, showing perfect white teeth. "Sound OK to me. Have never slept on train."

"Nor me," I admitted.

"Exactly my point," Dad replied, carefully taking

6

the pickle out of his burger. "And," he paused for effect, "this is no ordinary train. It's the Empire Builder and it's a double decker superliner. Coaches sixteen feet high. Upstairs and downstairs. It reminds me . . . oh drat!"

Dad realized he'd forgotten to look at the thermometer before shaking it down so he stuck it back in Rodney's mouth. "I can't figure out how Rodney missed his vaccination against Rubella," he muttered.

"It was that day the publisher called about doing a book on Napoleon," I reminded him. "You got talking and missed Rodney's appointment."

Dad looked guilty. "I think I remember it."

We chewed silently for a minute or two; then Rodney gulped. Dad took out the thermometer.

"Gee, Dad," wailed Rodney again.

"Sorry, Rodders." Dad rolled the thermometer this way and that. "Looks like a hundred," he said finally. "A day in bed is definitely called for."

Rodney tried to eat his food but couldn't swallow so Dad phoned room service for saltine crackers and a bottle of Sprite. I began to feel kind of sorry for my kid brother.

"I wish I was going with you guys," said Dad later that night as we settled in our beds. Rodney and he shared one bed, Nguyen and I the other by the window. As soon as Nguyen closed his brown eyes he was asleep.

"Ah yes," Dad continued, "the sound of metal wheels on the iron way, the hiss of steam in the cylinders. It's all part of your American heritage."

I leaned over and snapped out our lamp. "It's a diesel," I reminded him.

"Is it? Well the train is heated by steam. And you travel with all sorts of interesting people, strangers who meet, become friends, then part three days later, never to see each other again."

"Yes, Dad."

"And do you know what I like best about it?" I heard him pounding his pillow into a shape he liked. Rodney muttered to himself.

"No, Dad."

"It's completely safe. Nothing untoward *ever* happens on a train. You kids aren't likely to be hijacked to Cuba." He laughed.

"Very funny, Dad."

"I haven't forgotten that business at Loon Lake."

I knew that was coming. We had a cabin at Loon Lake in New Hampshire. Last summer we—Nguyen and I—and a girl called Jenny Weber—found these crooks smuggling precious art objects into Canada. With our help they were caught red-handed, but Dad about flipped his wig when he was told about it. Nguyen and I were confined to the back cabin while Rodney, who'd done nothing, got to fly over the lake in the Immigration Service helicopter.

8

"Well this time, there will be no excitement. Am I right Rodders?"

"Right, Dad."

I heard more settling sounds from the other bed and finally. "'Night boys."

Outside, the steadily falling snow muffled the sound of traffic, and the heavy curtain blocked out all the light. Still, I lay there for a long time trying to get to sleep. Nguyen always fell asleep immediately, but I couldn't. I wouldn't have admitted it for the world, but I was a bit scared. I'd never made a journey on my own. Maybe twelve is plenty old enough to go on a train alone, but two thousand miles?

Dad was snoring away, probably with his neck bent back the way he always slept. Normally he worried about us all the time. He was forever thinking wild animals would bite us and give us rabies. So if he wasn't worried, why should I be?

Jeez! If only I'd known.

2

The Empire Builder

THE NEXT DAY AFTER LUNCH DAD HELPED US INTO A Checker cab at the main doors of the Holiday Inn. It had stopped snowing; Nguyen and I had a suitcase each. Mine was a lightweight blue with plaid lining. Because the lock hadn't worked since Dad last fixed it, the case was held together with a worn leather belt. The handle was black from all the hands that had held it. I couldn't remember when we hadn't owned that case. Mom kept hiding it in the attic, but Dad always found it. Nguyen carried the new tan suitcase with a set of little wheels on one corner. He was the only person in the family who had the patience to pull the case without tipping it onto its side. So we made him use it.

Dad kissed both of us on the cheek right there in public and told us to be careful. We each had twenty-five bucks spending money, and Dad gave me five for the taxi and one to tip the attendant on the Empire Builder. The cab driver didn't pay any attention to us, he just waited and smoked a short cigar. The whole cab smelled of stale smoke.

As soon as we had finished waving to Dad I wound the window halfway down. The air was real cold, but it smelled fresher than the cigar smoke.

All the way to Union Station I kept looking at the meter. It was supposed to cost just about four dollars, and I had five. That was a very good tip according to Dad, but what was I to do if the bill was four sixty?

"Good thing Jenny not here," muttered Nguyen. "She take all the money for ice cream."

Boy, was he right. Jenny lived at Loon Lake and when she wasn't borrowing my bike she was ordering Tin Roofs with *our* money, making us settle for single scoops. Like all girls she was real bossy and . . . well the truth was Nguyen and I sort of got to like her in the end.

Chicago has a lot of skyscrapers, and we saw old buildings being knocked down everywhere. Even in the freezing cold men were working, erecting steel frames and laying bricks. Every time we came to a manhole cover, a great cloud of steam was coming out of it.

It was a relief when we reached the station.

"Four ten," said the driver.

I put the five dollar bill in the little tray in the glass

partition in front of me. The driver took it and came round to the trunk and took out our cases. Then he was gone.

"He a nice guy," said Nguyen, but I couldn't tell if he was serious.

I had on a jacket, ski cap, gloves and a set of ear muffs. It didn't help. I'd known cold days in Durham, but this was something else. It was like a cold knife cutting into me.

"Boy is it cold," I said.

"It not as cold as Japan," replied Nguyen who didn't seem to feel the cold the way I did, though when he spoke steam came out of his mouth. He had been evacuated there during the Vietnam war. No one knew if his folks were still alive or not. The International Red Cross was trying to find out. Nguyen didn't say much about them, and I sure didn't ask, but I knew he had an older sister and a twin brother. Neither of them had made it to the Japanese orphanage where Mom found Nguyen.

"Come on," I said to my brother who was staring up at the Sears Tower.

"I hope there no earthquakes here," he muttered more to himself than me. "It a long way to fall."

Not even Nguyen could balance the tan suitcase on its little wheels because there were bits of ice everywhere, and they got jammed in the wheels and tipped the case over. Finally he just carried it.

Dad had told us not to check our baggage. "You'll need your pajamas and toothbrushes," he said, as if we didn't know.

Now you might have thought Dad would be real upset about not going on the Empire Builder, what with all his talk about steam and railroad tracks and his model railway. The truth was, once he knew he couldn't go, Dad had got on the phone to some publisher in Chicago and spent an hour setting up a lunch meeting in the Holiday Inn's revolving restaurant on the thirty-third floor. He had wanted to go to Trader Vic's at the Palmer House, but he couldn't leave Rodney alone.

Dad is forever writing books on weird guys from olden times. Then he has to find somebody to publish them. Next fall we're moving to Ann Arbor because he has a new job. Somebody at the University of Michigan liked the book he wrote on the Roman Emperor, Titus. This guy was ruler for only two years. In that time Vesuvius blew its top and Titus flattened the Temple at Jerusalem. Then, according to Dad, he was poisoned by his brother. Can you believe Dad wrote four hundred pages about him? And then got a job offer—it didn't make any sense. Once we move, Mom is going to join the Detroit Symphony. We kids weren't consulted until it was all settled. Surprise! Anyway, we are going to keep the cottages at Loon Lake.

"I got cart," said Nguyen. It was one of those you

could use for a dollar. This one was just lying around so we got it free. It was real hard work at first, until we found a brake below the handle. Even then each wheel seemed to go in its own direction.

The lower level of the station was called the concourse. It had low ceilings and was jam packed with people, and the noise was deafening. On top of that there was a Salvation Army Band playing jazz—I'd thought they only played hymns. We passed lots of little stores. One advertised frozen packets of the "world's best chili" and another was selling posters of Henry Winkler as "The Fonz". Jeez! Even Rodney avoided *Happy Days* reruns. Talk about ancient!

We had to wait five minutes before the terminal gates opened. I had the tickets inside my jacket; Dad had fastened them there with a safety pin. Can you believe it? Just like when I was in kindergarten and had a note from the teacher.

A voice came over the loudspeaker; it bounced around the roof and was hard to understand. "Train Number 7, the Empire Builder, now ready for boarding. Seattle cars at the rear."

A flood of people jammed through the gates, pushing and shoving. The ticket inspector grinned as I handed ours over. "Reserved seats. Sixth car from the front." He returned the tickets; this time I put them in my coat pocket. "No carts on the platform, boys."

Nguyen pushed the cart out of the way while I

waited impatiently. I was anxious to get on the train. Nguyen's suitcase ran fine along the platform, and I was soon puffing as I hurried to keep up.

Clouds of steam were hissing out from under the cars. They came from pipes that heated the train. The cars looked as if they were on fire, and several passengers seemed to vanish as they walked into the steam and climbed aboard.

Boy, were those cars high! They were real high! Not like the trains we have back East. They were double deckers, as Dad had said, with two sets of windows, one above the other. Silver cars with red, white and blue trim.

We passed a bunch of people all kissing and hugging farewell and jumping up and down to keep warm. Their faces were blue, and quite a few were drinking from paper cups.

"This our car," Nguyen called out. "Number 32002."

When we got to the door, a man in a blue uniform stepped out of the door onto the platform. He wore a peaked cap and the biggest set of whiskers I'd ever seen. His face just seemed covered in bright red hair. He wore a blue nameplate with "Hank Lomax" on it.

I fished out our tickets—they were sort of crumpled. Mr. Lomax smoothed them out, grinned and tore off the ends. "Two high-steppin' gents traveling alone, eh?"

"Yes," I said, longing to get in out of the cold.

"Not cold are you?" he asked. He shook his head; the whiskers quivered. "Wait 'til we reach North Dakota. You boys need anything just yell for Hank or push the button."

He stood to one side. "In you go, Room 12, this level, just round the stairs. Now look out!"

A baggage cart came out of the steam and almost clipped the back of my suitcase. A girl with long hair flying behind was driving it. She grinned and waved as she went by. It was a three wheeler, piled high with luggage, and the engine gave out that high-pitched whine you get with electric motors.

I gave Mr. Lomax a dollar tip. He took off his cap, scratched his head and stared at the dollar bill for a long time. Then he said, "Well, thank you kindly, Sir." He seemed to be grinning, but Dad had said, "Don't call the attendant a porter, and give him a dollar tip." So I did.

The stairs didn't come down to the platform; Mr. Lomax had placed a small stool below the bottom step, and he helped Nguyen and me climb aboard. When we were both inside he handed our suitcases up. I passed the one with wheels to my brother and carried the other.

The inside of the car was enormous, almost like being in a house. There was carpeting, a dark green color, and it also covered the walls. I peeped up the stairs but couldn't see much.

Nguyen was already in our room by the time I got there. The window faced the platform, and there were two wide seats facing each other. A little table was fixed to the bottom of the window frame and above the window was an upper bunk.

Of course both of us wanted the top berth. If I'd been with Rodney it would have been the old story. When Dad took us anywhere by car, Rodney wanted the front seat. He always tried to sneak out and get into the car before I did. Dad had a '78 Olds Cutlass with two doors. If it wasn't unlocked, we'd both have to wait until Dad got in on the driver's side, then fight over it.

Well, I didn't want to fight with Nguyen; whenever Rodney and I got into it, Dad always said it was "bush" to fight over the front seat.

"We toss for it?" Nguyen suggested.

"OK," I replied, and called, "heads." It was tails so I lost. What's new?

"I sleep there tonight, you tomorrow," said Nguyen.

Boy, I like to think I'd be that generous!

It didn't take long to inspect the rest of our room; there was a sink, a toilet, and a small shower.

From a small speaker in the ceiling there was music. It was the same kind you get in elevators. It isn't by anybody, and you don't remember any of it a minute or so later. Nguyen turned it off.

We found a place for our coats and suitcases, then sat and looked out of the window. It was only two o'clock, but already it seemed to be getting darker. Still, there was something great about sitting in a warm place looking out at a cold world. Soon, I could see only my own reflection looking back at me so I leaned close to the glass and cupped my hands around my face to get a real look.

The people with the paper cups were still there. Out of the steam and gloom behind them came a man in a red uniform pushing a cart on which was a large suitcase. By his side was an old man with a white moustache, wearing a long grey coat with the collar turned up. Around his neck was a grey scarf. A black fur hat was jammed down over his ears, but tufts of white hair stuck out to the sides. He walked fast, though he was bent over and using a cane.

I didn't see any more. My breath misted up the window.

"You want explore the train?" asked Nguyen. He had already pulled out his pocket chess set and a book by Bobby Fischer. He had most of the games memorized!

Well, I had planned to be cool on this trip. Exploring the train was pretty dumb; it was the sort of thing Rodney would do—if Dad went with him. On the other hand, I'd only been on a train once before, and never one with an upstairs, and there wasn't anyone around to complain. "OK," I said.

We went up the carpeted steps to the upper level. At the top we saw the old man still wearing his outdoor clothes. Mr. Lomax was helping him.

"Deluxe Bedroom E, you say?" the man asked in a hoarse voice.

"Just to your left, Sir."

"My associate, Mr. Nicholas Drake, will be along later. He's always late, confound him."

"Right, Mr. Kurtz. I'll see he finds you."

Mr. Lomax caught sight of us and winked; I was relieved. For a moment I thought he'd tell us to go back to our room.

There was no connection between cars on the bottom level. There were four rooms like ours and two larger ones. To get from one car to the next, we had to go upstairs, where Mr. Kurtz's room was, walk along a corridor, open a door, and step into a short passage connecting the cars. The noise out there was much louder, and it was a lot colder because of the metal plates under our feet.

We counted the cars as we went through the train. Next to ours was another sleeper, then a lounge car, with seats like those on an airplane but with footrests. Then came a car with a counter in the middle; the aisle wound around it, and a bunch of people were standing around ordering drinks from an attendant in a bright red apron.

The next three cars were ordinary coaches. Then came a sleeper and the two cars going to Seattle. We went up and down some stairs, but there wasn't much to see except people settling in and a few babies yelling. So we started trekking back the way we came, past our car toward the front.

The front of the train was much more interesting. We passed Mr. Kurtz's room; now a "Do Not Disturb" sign was hanging from the door handle.

The next car was the sightseer lounge car. There were windows everywhere, and single armchairs facing out with swivel bases. There was a piano too. Nguyen played a few notes. "Need tuning," he said. I remember Mom saying that when she met him in the orphanage she'd been amazed to find he had perfect pitch.

Nguyen disappeared down the stairs. A minute later he was back.

"Snack bar and card game," he reported. "They wanted me to play."

Boy, would they have learned a lesson! Not only is Nguyen the world's best mah-jongg player, but when it comes to cards he can remember every one that's been played.

Next was the dining car. It was like a restaurant. Each table had a white cloth and a vase holding a single red rose; waiters were bustling around arranging napkins and cutlery.

A man carrying menus under his arm saw us. "Nothing more to see, boys," he said. "Three more cars and the baggage car. Better get back to your seats, we'll be leaving soon."

We turned back the way we'd come. There was a sudden jolt; I steadied myself against a table, then followed Nguyen down the car.

The announcer's voice came over the loudspeaker system. "The Empire Builder, Chicago, St. Paul, Portland, Seattle Superliner Service, now leaving Chicago Union Station at 2:30 P.M. Our time of arrival in Portland, 8:35 A.M., in Seattle, 9:15 A.M. on Thursday."

We stopped briefly in the sightseer car. I checked my watch. It was 2:28. Outside, we could see a man in a short raincoat and a hat with a tiny feather in the hatband. He was holding a small suitcase in his right hand and wore dark glasses even though the platform was gloomy as night. He was waving his arms and, though we couldn't hear him, he seemed to be bawling out a baggage attendant who was struggling to push a huge steamer trunk toward the baggage car. As the attendant moved out of sight, the man in dark glasses looked after him intently. Then he turned to the train and boarded, in the nick of time.

The train began to move; there were several quick jerks, then a sudden forward movement. I grabbed for the seat beside me. Outside the platform seemed to be moving backwards. Below us, people waved frantically at friends and relatives as the Empire Builder pulled slowly out of the station into the gloomy December afternoon. Outside, there was the low mournful sound of a diesel horn. Our long journey had begun.

3

---◘━◘━━━━━━◘━◘---

Mrs. Agnes Larkin

THE FACES OF THE PEOPLE WAVING GOODBYE BECAME
a blur as the Empire Builder, its horn sounding, turned
in a wide curve and headed north.

When we opened the door to pass to the next car,
the noise increased sharply. The space between the
cars wasn't soundproofed; the metal plates underfoot
were constantly shifting and very cold. It was a relief to
slide back the doors and enter our own regular, warm
car—even though it, too, now swayed gently from side
to side.

Just as we reached the stairs leading down to our
room, a man started up them. It was the man in dark
glasses who'd almost missed the train while seeing to his
trunk.

"You kids wait until I get up," he said sharply, with a scowl. "And why aren't you in your seats?"

We waited until he reached the top of the stairs. "And don't make a lot of noise," he added "Mr. Kurtz doesn't want to be disturbed by noisy brats charging up and down these stairs."

The train rocked suddenly. His glasses fell to the ground. Nguyen bent down to pick them up as the man grabbed a guardrail to steady himself.

"Give me those," he said, snatching the sunglasses from Nguyen. Then he pushed past us into the deluxe bedroom ignoring the "Do Not Disturb" sign. The door was unlocked, and we heard a hoarse voice exclaim. "About time, Nicholas Drake, about time."

The door slammed shut. Nguyen whispered to me as we climbed downstairs. "Mr. Drake in hot water now."

"Good," I replied, opening our door and settling into my seat. "Let's get out Dad's map so we can follow the route. I've seen enough of Nicholas Drake."

Nguyen grinned. Nothing ever fazed him. Rummaging through the suitcase, he pulled out the map with Dad's comments and our route traced in green ink. He'd spent two evenings on it, and now he wasn't going to see any of the sights marked on it. Nguyen put his chess set on one of the suitcases and unfolded the map.

I glanced out of the window. The neighborhood

was pretty grubby. In the distance, the Sears Tower and another skyscraper with two TV antennas on its roof towered over everything. It wasn't snowing, but the sky was the color of lead.

Going north, the Empire Builder followed Lake Michigan which was hidden from us by grimy buildings. Still, I looked at them because it's always interesting to see what you're not supposed to see. Lots of them had faded old advertising signs—"Smoke Mail Pouch Tobacco" and such. One offered Coca-Cola for five cents a bottle. I'll bet even Dad wasn't old enough to remember those days.

Ten minutes later we pulled into Glenview. It was beginning to snow and, as far as I could see, there was only one person on the platform, a tiny woman with two small suitcases. She wore a blue coat almost down to her ankles. Peeping out under the coat were the toes of fur boots. Most surprising was a red ski mask that covered most of her face except for her granny glasses. She was smoking a cigarette. From the way the snow covered her, it seemed as if she hadn't moved for quite a while.

Mr. Lomax got off the train and placed his stool beneath the steps. The little old lady walked slowly toward him, and he went to meet her, taking the two suitcases. As he passed our window, I saw that one of them was a portable typewriter.

He stowed the suitcase and typewriter on board,

then came back to help the lady up the steps. She dropped her cigarette and stepped on it. She had the smallest feet I'd ever seen, even with the fur boots on.

Seconds later, the attendant had picked up his stool and signaled to the engineer. We heard the moan of the diesel whistle followed by a thud as the door closed. The platform slid away from us, and we were on our way again.

Nguyen glanced up from his chess set. "You want to go to the lounge, Jeff?"

"Why not?" I said, relieved he hadn't wanted to play chess. "Bring the map."

When we got there, it was pretty crowded, but we managed to find two seats at the far end. The Empire Builder made occasional short stops, and it wasn't long before there was an announcement that we were approaching Milwaukee. All I could see were dirty buildings and factories. When the snow wasn't falling hard, I could see people moving around inside them.

Nguyen went downstairs and got two Classic Cokes.

"Sorry they only got cans, Jeff," he said, "and they seventy-five cents each."

That was too bad, the can bit especially, because no matter what anyone says, I can always taste the aluminum.

The train ran smoothly. I'd heard all that stuff

about the tracks being pretty bad so I thought we'd be crawling along, but everything flew by as we headed west. Now and again when the track curved we could see the whole length of the train in each direction.

We were leaving the cities behind us and crossing fields and passing through little towns with wooden houses painted white. Some even had picket fences. The few people who were forced to wait while we crossed their main streets seemed happy to see us because they generally waved.

I don't know how long Nguyen and I sat there. As the train settled into a rhythm, I found myself looking at our reflections in the window. Nguyen was much stockier than me; I was two inches taller, and it was strange to think we were brothers. Dad was more like Nguyen though they weren't related at all really. I was more like Mom, a bit on the skinny side and with the same fair skin and light brown hair.

I wondered what Nguyen was thinking on a train thousands of miles from where he was born and not knowing if any of his family were still alive. He seldom mentioned them so we didn't either.

Maybe he caught me looking at his reflection because suddenly he said, "I pretty hungry, Jeff."

There had been one announcement about early dinner. I hadn't paid any attention because I figured we'd go to the Amcafe car and get a burger or something. However when the announcer said dinner was being served, I decided we'd go to the dining car. So I told Nguyen.

"Maybe it a little expensive," he said doubtfully.

"Let's go," I said, standing up and leading the way to the stairs.

The train had its own rhythm. At first the swaying had been tricky. I felt like a sailor on a ship, but pretty soon we could move quickly just by resting our hands lightly on the top of seats for a little steadying as we walked through the compartments.

We passed through the corridor between the cars and slid back the dining car door. I almost lost my nerve. At least half the tables were full, and waiters with towels over their arms were serving people like a real restaurant. Mr. Kurtz, still wrapped in his coat, was just leaving by the far door, leaning heavily on his cane. The man in charge, I think he's called the maître d', came over and said, "This way, please."

We had to follow, but he didn't seat us at an empty table. Instead, he put us at a table with the little old lady I'd seen getting on at Glenview. Sitting bolt upright with a large wine list in front of her, she didn't seem to notice us.

When we were seated, I sipped ice water from a goblet. The waiter gave Nguyen and me menus. The lady lowered the wine list and peered at us over the top of her glasses.

"The filet of sole is to be avoided at all costs," she

said. For a small woman she had a loud voice; I felt people turning around to look at us, so I fixed my eyes on the rose in the center of the table.

"At all costs," she repeated in case we'd missed it. "Never eat fish on a train."

Nguyen didn't say anything. She stared at me as if challenging me to argue. I didn't.

"You're new to train travel, aren't you?"

"Yes," I said.

"Thought so. Your names?"

Boy was she nosy! "Jeff Glover," I answered; "this is my brother Nguyen."

"Agnes Larkin, pleased to meet you." She stuck out her hand, and we shook. "The name means nothing to you?"

I shook my head.

"Extraordinary. What does the younger generation do these days? Surely you've read *Castle D'eth?*"

I shook my head again.

"Or *The Last Breath of Roger St. Simeon? Terror Track? The Murder of Mable Dunnin?*"

I didn't dare shake my head. Out of the corner of my eye I saw Nguyen's face; his eyes were as large as saucers. Quickly, he looked into his menu.

"You have to fill in slips when you order. I'll do it for you, boys." She checked things rapidly with a pencil, then sat back and sighed. A waiter approached. Mrs. Larkin said. "No wine. There's nothing special about

Mateus Rosé. We'll all have the same thing," she added. "Steaks, medium rare, baked potato, sour cream with chives, tossed salads, vinegar and oil for them. Waldorf for me. More ice water to drink now. Coffee with the blueberry cheesecake, extra cream, extra sugar."

She handed the waiter her wine list and menu. He took ours. I hadn't even opened mine!

"On trains they seat you with other people. I like it; it's very friendly. America is the only country in the world where restaurants make people wait until there is an empty table. Not, however, on Amtrak."

Mrs. Larkin was about the oddest person I'd ever met. She didn't look *too* strange. I mean she was dressed like an old woman would dress in a sort of matching suit with a little pink hat. She had one of those cameo things on her blouse, and the fur boots of course.

I'd noticed an accent. "You're English aren't you?" I asked.

Mrs. Larkin glared at me. "I am not," she said loudly. A couple at the table on my left looked over at us. I wanted the ground to open and swallow me up.

"I am from New Zealand which is as far from England as you can get. Not that I have anything against England. Some of the best crimes in the world took place there."

"Jack the Kipper," said Nguyen.

"Eh?" said Mrs. Larkin.

"Jack the Kipper, saw it on TV."

"*Ripper*, boy. Jack the *Ripper*. Priceless! For heaven's sake haven't you heard of Palmer the Poisoner, John Reginald Halliday Christie, Hague the Acid Bath Murderer?"

Nguyen shook his head, fixing his eyes on the table cloth. "The poor boy looks in his menu. Thinks of kippers for breakfast and confuses Jack with a salted fish." She dug in her purse and took out a pack of cigarettes, then glancing at us, dropped them back. "Better not," she muttered to herself. "Bad example to the young."

We passed a small station painted white with a sign saying "Wisconsin Dells."

"The Dells," she said, "rock worn into strange shapes by the river. This is double track, automatic block signal territory."

Boy, that sounded familiar. "My dad had a model railroad. He talked about blocks all the time," I said.

Mrs. Larkin stared at me and said nothing.

"You sure know a lot about trains," said Nguyen after a long pause.

"Trains and murder," she replied. "Never travel any other way if possible, never write about anything else. Never fly unless absolutely necessary. Weren't made to fly. If we'd been meant to fly we'd have had wings like the angels instead of shoulder blades."

There was a quick glimpse of a river as the train crossed a high trestle bridge. In the distance we saw the rock twisted and hollowed into wild shapes.

The salads arrived. I don't like salads much, but I was starving. Mrs. Larkin's salad seemed to be made of bits of apple and raisins.

Even the napkins had the Amtrak symbol on them. Nguyen was absently tracing his knife around the pattern while waiting for his steak.

Underneath was written, "Nice to have you with us."

"I gave them that slogan," said Mrs. Larkin, who didn't miss anything. "Felt a need to keep American railways alive."

The steak was pretty good when it arrived; we didn't eat that many at home. Only when Dad sold a book.

"Not bad," Mrs. Larkin said. "After all, they've only got a microwave. At least better than airplane food."

The waiter had been standing nearby, and he seemed real happy when he heard this.

When the cheesecake arrived, the waiter turned over our cups and slipped a piece of paper between them and the saucers. I soon saw why. Coffee slopped over the top of the cup even on the smoothest curves.

The blueberry cheesecake was great. It's my favorite flavor for one thing. Nguyen and I even managed half a cup of coffee apiece. We sure didn't want to offend Mrs. Larkin.

She looked at her coffee cup gently swaying with the motion of the train. "Better than it used to be," she said suddenly, "before the new welded track, these coaches swayed like fairground rides. Coffee slopped everywhere. One million dollars they cost, and they rode like Dodg'em cars."

She paused. Out of the corner of my eye, I saw Mr. Drake enter the car. He was placed at the next table, which was empty. When he saw us, he scowled.

The waiter approached him. Mrs. Larkin sat back in her chair so she could hear. Jeez! She was as nosy as she was bossy.

She leaned forward when the waiter left and sipped her coffee. Then she put the cup down, reached into her purse and said. "My treat."

I didn't see the bill, but I did see a twenty and some fives on the table. Boy, we'd think twice before we ate there again. Mrs. Larkin stood up and left with us trailing behind.

Outside the dining car she stopped.

"Do you know that man?"

"His name Nicholas Drake," said Nguyen. "He work for Mr. Kurtz."

"I don't like him. I don't like his looks. And for another thing," she peered around as if afraid of being overheard. "Not only did he order fish, he ordered a red wine to go with it."

Straightening up, she stared first at me then at my brother. "Boys, there's going to be trouble on this journey. Take my word for it. I can sense these things. And I'm never wrong. Never!"

4

Mr. Kurtz Vanishes

IT STARTED THAT VERY NIGHT.

After we left the dining car, Mrs. Larkin led the way to our room. She had the one next door.

"It was the best they could do," she said, looking at the door. "Number 14. I didn't get on at Chicago, so I suppose I was lucky to get anything."

She unlocked her door and said, "Good night boys," over her shoulder and was gone.

"Phew, that some bossy lady," said Nguyen when we were safely behind our locked door. "I not go to New Zealand."

"I thought she was crazy at first," I admitted. Actually, I was a bit afraid she was one of those people you're always being told not to get in cars with. "But she was OK."

34

Nguyen started to look at the map; it was so big it hung over the edge of the table. He refolded it and found the green line Dad had drawn on it.

"We soon come . . ." he began but stopped as the train suddenly plunged into darkness.

"A tunnel," I finished for him.

"Well, it called Tunnel City," he said, as we rushed through the town.

Nguyen carefully folded up the map and put it away. He is always real tidy. Then he got out his chess set and put the pieces out carefully and began to play a game from Bobby Fischer's book.

I watched for a while, then turned and peered into the darkness outside. A mirror image of me stared back at me. Beyond, it was snowing, a white sheet as far as the eye could see covering everything.

The Empire Builder rushed on; I was so used to the sound of the wheels on the tracks, that I didn't hear them unless I made a conscious effort to listen. Only once in a great while did the diesel horn sound—usually when a freight passed going in the opposite direction. Then there would be a sudden explosion of sound and the windows rattled. I'd had my forehead pressed against the cold glass when the last freight passed, and I felt the vibration. When I tried to count the cars, they were gone too fast.

At first it was fun just sitting there, gliding through

35

the night towards Mom. We were warm and cozy while everything outside was frozen.

Nguyen looked up, grinned and put away his chess set. "Bobby sacrifice a queen and still win. He some player. Maybe better than Karpov. Maybe the best ever."

The miles shot by. I didn't want to go to bed, but I was eager to see what the bunks were like. The best thing was there wasn't anyone to tell us to go to bed. Now we could stay up until morning if we wanted to. I really liked that. We hadn't been allowed to stay up much past midnight even on the Webelos overnight with the Cub Scouts.

"When we go to bed?" asked Nguyen, as if he could read my thoughts.

"Dunno," I said.

Nguyen fetched the map, unfolded it and said, "What about St. Paul? It a big station."

"When do we get there?"

"Ten thirty-five, depart eleven five. Dad write time on map."

"OK," I said, "but now I want a Coke."

We climbed up the stairs. Instead of going to the lounge car, we walked down the train to the Amcafe car. We got to be pretty good at walking through the cars without holding on. Cokes were a nickel cheaper than in the machines.

"Two beers?" asked the attendant. Adults always

think that's funny. I tasted beer once at Dad's fish fry, and you couldn't pay me to drink the stuff.

"Two Cokes," I said, giving him a dollar bill and two quarters.

"Coming up," he said.

They were in cans so I asked for a paper cup.

"No charge," the attendant said, giving me one and a dime.

We decided to stay in the Amcafe car. It was almost deserted. One man sat in his chair with a jacket over his face, and there was a fat balding man reading a paperback book about Berlin.

Nguyen was trying to get the top off his can when the tab broke. That meant we had to jam the tab in with a quarter. The Coke fizzed around the edges, and when he tried to drink almost nothing came out.

"I'll take it," I said, reaching for it. "You take mine."

It took a long time for the Coke to fill my cup, but we weren't in any hurry. It was strange to think that Dad was still in Chicago with Rodney. The day after tomorrow, they'd be waiting for us in Oregon.

The train pulled into La Crosse. Through the snow we could see the cold dark water of the Mississippi beneath us as we crossed into Minnesota.

"Boy, I'd sure hate to fall in there," I said.

"Me too," said Nguyen finishing his Coke and setting the can down next to him on the seat and looking at his watch. "We ten minutes late."

We stayed there until 8:30. Though I hated to admit it, I was getting pretty bored. Once the newness of going on the Empire Builder wore off, it wasn't much better than traveling by bus, except there was much more room.

On the way back to our room we decided to look into the sightseer car. It was crammed with people. Everyone was talking, the piano was being pounded to death, and the room was full of smoke.

"This place really skipping," said Nguyen, as we backed out, heading for our room.

"Jumping," I corrected, "but at least we won't hear that racket in our room."

"It not please Mr. Kurtz if he come up here."

We didn't stop long in St. Paul. Since we were almost twenty minutes behind schedule, the announcer urged everyone to hurry along.

The snow had stopped falling, and as we left the station I could see a large floodlit building with a dome on top in the distance. That was all we got to see of St. Paul.

The Empire Builder looped back over the Mississippi. Nguyen glanced at his watch. "Almost eight hours," he said, "and we've come just over four hundred miles."

"Let's get my bed fixed," I said, standing up.

It wasn't as easy as I thought. The table had to be stowed away, then the facing seats pushed very firmly together so they flattened out to form the lower berth.

The upper bed was already in position. Standing on the bottom bed, Nguyen handed down my bedding, then made up his own.

"How are you going to climb up there?" I said. "There must be an easier way. How do old people get up?"

Nguyen found the answer. One of the armrests doubled as a two-step ladder.

We put on pajamas, brushed our teeth and got into bed. Nguyen had his book on chess, and I was reading *Aliens* again. There were these little lights in the wall you could aim directly at the page. Of course, any time you moved, you couldn't see a thing.

I soon got tired of reading and turned off the light, lying there with the blind open, watching the world go by.

The mattress was a bit too soft, but the linen was cool and crisp, and the blanket warm. There was even a small blue night light, so Rodney would have been OK on the Empire Builder. He still slept with a night light —one of those dumb things with a scorpion frozen in plastic. Just above my head was a neat little pocket where his glasses would fit. Boy this train was built for Rodneys.

The one thing that worried me was accidentally

pressing the attendant button in my sleep. I sure didn't want to call in Mr. Lomax at two a.m. and have to tell him it was a mistake.

I found it difficult to go to sleep at once. My senses seemed much more acute as I lay there. I heard Mrs. Larkin next door as she occasionally bumped against the wall. Footsteps passed near our door more than once, and there were voices as people went down the stairs into the bathrooms.

But eventually the warm bed, the gentle swaying of the car, and the exhaustion from excitement proved too much. I had a vague memory of a click as Nguyen turned off his light, and once the horn sounded softly. I drifted off.

The next thing I knew, there was a loud bumping on the stairs outside our room. Voices were raised, and I recognized them immediately even though I was still sleepy.

"Ruined!" Mr. Kurtz shouted in his hoarse voice. "You know they'll find out I took that money."

There was more banging against the wall of our room. I got out of bed and moved to the door, opening it slightly. I felt Nguyen by my side. There was light from the bulbs in the ceiling but both men were hidden from us by the stairs.

"It's all right," Mr. Drake was saying in a soothing voice. "You'll put the money back on Monday."

"No, it's too late!" There was the sound of a door opening, and a blast of ice cold air and wet snowflakes was sucked into the car and whirled around the stairs. The engine noise was a continuous roar. Then above it came a loud shriek.

Mr. Drake's voice was filled with terror. "Mr. Kurtz, Mr. Kurtz!"

We ran around the stairs to the entrance of the car. Mr. Drake was hanging on to the edge of the door frame, his head outside the coach. Already snow covered his dark blue suit and the carpeting. Snow immediately blew into my face, and the cold bit into my cheeks. It wasn't pitch dark outside, and an emergency light shone down from the roof above us. Through the door I could see nothing but an endless stretch of dark snow.

Of Mr. Kurtz, there was no sign.

5

Mrs. Larkin Is Suspicious

WITH AN EFFORT, MR. DRAKE DREW HIS HEAD BACK into the coach, his hair covered with snow. The wind outside was howling and flurries of snow swirled around us. "He jumped from the train," he said, looking at us. "I couldn't stop him. He just jumped." He was shouting to be heard.

Nguyen acted quickly. Reaching up for the emergency handle, he pulled it down.

There was a loud squealing of brakes, and the train shuddered. I don't know how long the train kept going, but it was a long time. The wheels screeched along the track and hundreds of sparks mixed with the snow outside.

The Empire Builder finally lurched to a halt, knocking us to the floor. Nguyen let out a shout of pain.

He fell on top of me. When I got into a sitting position, I saw him staggering to his feet. When he took his hand from his head, there was blood on it.

A familiar voice came from behind us. "Boys, what on earth's going on?"

I looked up. Mrs. Larkin, dressed in a blue robe and wearing a scarf over curlers, was looking round the corner.

"It's Mr. Kurtz," said Nguyen. "Mr. Kurtz, he dead."

Mrs. Larkin stared beyond him into the empty landscape. I realized I was shivering, and it wasn't just from the cold.

"You OK?" I asked Nguyen.

"Hit head when train stop."

Mrs. Larkin took off her scarf. "Hold this to it, Nguyen. Chances are it's a clean cut."

Lots of things happened quickly after that. Mr. Lomax and a huge black man came around the corner. The attendant was talking into his walkie-talkie. He put it down when he saw the open door, edged past us and pulled on a handle. The doors slid shut, there was a final icy blast, then almost at once it felt warmer.

"What's going on?" he demanded. "Who opened the door?"

"Ask him," said Mrs. Larkin, pointing to Mr. Drake. "He can tell you. I've got to attend to this boy's head."

By now people had gathered on the stairs and some were crowding around the corner to see what was going on.

"We can't talk here," said Mr. Lomax. "Sergeant, do you mind settling those people down. Just say it was an accidental brake release."

The black man turned and began moving people back up the stairs.

"You've got to hurry," I said. "Mr. Kurtz jumped off the train back there."

"Jumped off?"

"Yes!" I was shouting now. "We've got to look for him."

Mr. Lomax turned away and began talking into his walkie-talkie. Mr. Drake was leaning against the wall, using the side of the car to steady himself.

"All right, all right," Mr. Lomax said. "I've radioed for a helicopter from the Air Force base. It'll be here in a few minutes, and if Mr. Kurtz is out there, they'll find him. Now come with me."

He led us past the bathrooms to a locked room. Selecting a key from a bunch on a chain around his waist, he opened the door. The room was twice the size of ours.

"Everyone sit down," he ordered. "There's water for the boy's head."

Mrs. Larkin took Nguyen to the sink. "It's just a cut," she said. "Very clean." She sounded relieved.

Then, Mr. Lomax opened one of the cupboards and took down a box with a red cross on it. Mrs. Larkin took it from him. "I'll attend to the boy. It's just a matter of cutting a little hair and cleaning the wound."

I guess when you're as old as Mrs. Larkin you've pretty much done everything sometime in your life. Anyway, she sure seemed to know what she was doing. "Now," said Mr. Lomax, "what happened?" He looked at Mr. Drake who was sitting on the edge of one of the beds; he licked his lips several times before he spoke.

"Mr. Kurtz is the Chairman of the Board of Intellikom. It's a communications company—one of the big five. I'm the chief accountant. Just this morning, I discovered over a million dollars was unaccounted for. I asked Mr. Kurtz if I could discuss an urgent matter with him on the way to the board meeting in Portland."

"Well?" said Mr. Lomax, impatiently.

"I told Mr. Kurtz what I knew. After all, as chief accountant I must protect myself." He turned to all of us. "I mean, the money is my responsibility."

"Of course," agreed Mr. Lomax, "but what happened?"

"We checked over the figures for hours and hours. Then suddenly he went completely to pieces. Said I'd ruined him." The accountant hesitated, then continued. "What I didn't realize until that moment was that Mr. Kurtz had taken the money. I never thought he would embezzle from his own company. I mean

45

... I mean ..." his voice trailed away. He began to sob gently, took out a handkerchief and blew his nose. We waited until he could continue.

"And then he ran out of the bedroom, down the stairs saying he would kill himself rather than suffer the disgrace and spend his life in prison. I grabbed him at the bottom of the stairs, that's when we bumped into the boys' wall. I tried to reason with him, but he broke loose from me, opened the door with the emergency handle and jumped." He blew his nose again.

Mrs. Larkin was sitting on one of the seats looking closely at Mr. Drake as he spoke. She was shaking her head very slightly, and her lips were pursed.

"And you couldn't stop him?" she asked.

"I tried to, but he had the door open before I realized ..."

In the distance we heard a throbbing beating sound. It grew louder. Through one of the windows, I caught a brief glimpse of a powerful searchlight crossing the snow towards us. For an instant, the whole bedroom was bathed in white light. Then the helicopter roared overhead, and was gone.

"They'll soon find him," said Mr. Lomax. Mrs. Larkin gave a loud sniff as she stuck a Band-Aid on Nguyen's head.

"You can go back to your rooms now; you boys get into bed immediately or you'll catch your death. You be sure to watch that cut," Mr. Lomax cautioned Nguyen, rising and going to the door. "I'll radio the engineer; nothing more we can do."

"Get dressed," Mrs. Larkin said to us, when we were out of earshot.

"Dressed?" I said. "What for?"

"Something's not quite right," she muttered. "We need a council of war."

Nguyen and I went back to our room. I put on my jeans and a sweater. I didn't know why I was getting dressed, and I sure didn't know why we were taking orders from some old lady we hardly knew.

The train began to move, at first it seemed to be straining. The motion was jerky, then it settled down as the Empire Builder built up its speed.

There was a sharp, double rap on the door. I didn't even check first—who could it be but Mrs. Larkin?

She was dressed in a dark green pantsuit, and there weren't any curlers in her hair. She was carrying three cans of Coke.

"Well," she said, sitting on the bottom bunk between us and fiddling with the tab on her can, "what do you think?"

"Think?" I asked.

"Think. About Nicholas Drake's story."

"What about it?" I said.

"A man jumps off a train in the middle of nowhere, and you don't find that strange?"

She was fiddling with the tab still. Finally, Nguyen

47

took the can from her and opened it up. I studied my reflection in the window.

She glanced at me, then Nguyen. "Hrumph," she said, "let me tell you boys something. I am known as the Agatha Christie of New Zealand," she added. "I suppose you've heard of *her*? I've written twenty-three crime novels, won six awards including two Edgars, and I've never heard such drivel in my life." She took a long drink from her can. "Never!"

"Mr. Lomax seemed to believe it," I said.

"He's a train person—not a student of the criminal mind." She got up, walked across the room and turned to face us. "However, feeling something and proving it . . . they're quite different. Quite different."

"When they find Mr. Kurtz, he'll be able to tell them what happened," I suggested.

She shook her head. "No, Jeff. As Nguyen so quaintly put it, 'Mr. Kurtz, he dead.' Mr. Lomax didn't want you to know, but a man would freeze to death in minutes out there. The snow would cover his body, and if they're lucky they'll find the body in the spring thaw. Unless . . ."

"Unless what?" asked Nguyen.

"Unless the wild animals get him first."

I shuddered. So Mr. Kurtz really was dead after all.

"We heard it all," I told her. "The argument, the struggle, all of it."

"It's a puzzle," she admitted. "But there's something not quite right about this whole business. Wish I could put my finger on it. Did you see them come aboard?"

"Sure," I said. "At Chicago."

"Together?"

I looked at Nguyen. "No," he said, "they each came alone."

"Right," I said. "Mr. Drake had a big trunk too. He put it in the baggage car."

Mrs. Larkin dug in her purse, took out a pack of cigarettes, glanced at us, sighed, and put them back.

"They came aboard separately?"

"Yes."

Nguyen turned to me. I looked at him. Nobody said anything.

At last Mrs. Larkin broke the silence. "Why did Mr. Drake make this trip?"

"He had business . . . with Mr. Kurtz," I said. "He told us that."

Nguyen looked as though he might say something. I knew the signs—he was thinking, and it wasn't about chess. Mrs. Larkin also noticed him. "Come on boy, spit it out."

Nguyen fixed his eyes on the floor. "Mr. Drake say he come on train to speak to Mr. Kurtz."

"About the missing money," I said.

Nguyen's eyes hadn't moved. "Yet he got no brief-case."

"Of course not," I pointed out. "He had a trunk and a suitcase."

Then it struck me, but Nguyen put it into words. "Why would man bring trunk and a suitcase when he was only going to talk about some accounts? Mr. Drake look as if he going on world cruise."

Mrs. Larkin had got to her feet and was almost shaking with excitement. "You're a very smart boy Nguyen. You should take up writing—once you've mastered the language."

In her excitement, Mrs. Larkin had shaken up her Coke; it began to fizz through the hole and trickle down the sides. Nguyen took it from her and put it in the sink.

Mrs. Larkin's eyes were positively shining. "Let's go," she said. "Let's go."

"Go," I repeated. "Go where?"

She stared at me as if I was crazy. "Where? Why the baggage car of course. I want to see what's in that mysterious trunk!"

6

===o=o=========o=o===

The Steamer Trunk

RIGHT THEN I KNEW MRS. LARKIN HAD NEVER HAD ANY kids. I could just see Dad telling us we were going to look in the baggage car of a train at six in the morning. And my brother with a cut on the head!

"Meet me outside," she said, "I'll get my torch."

"Torch?" said Nguyen.

"Flashlight, boy, flashlight. Oh, be sure to put on sweaters."

When she was safely out of the room I said to Nguyen, "We can't go messing around in that baggage car this time of morning."

Nguyen was struggling into his thick wool sweater. I guess that was his answer. My Aunt Gertrude had knitted it for him because she figured he'd always be cold, coming from the tropics. It was the very first gift he'd received in the States so he treasured it. It sort of made me feel guilty because when I heard Nguyen was coming to live with us, I wasn't too happy about it. Rodney was one thing, a kid brother you can always ignore, but Nguyen was just about my age. Also he didn't speak much English, so at first Dad and Mom talked to him in French, which left me out.

He had pulled his head through the neck of the sweater and was wrestling with the arms. He stopped and looked at me. "Mrs. Larkin not take 'no' for an answer."

He was right of course.

Nguyen struggled violently, swinging his arms up and down. The sweater was a year old but it still sagged in places. My aunt vaguely remembered my age and size, but my brother was shorter. The sleeves had to be pushed back on his wrists, but the chest with its pink flamingoes was tight.

"It very ironic," said Nguyen. "If Dad say not to go to baggage car, we want to go. Mrs. Larkin say go, we don't want to."

"Right," I muttered, pulling on my Oilers hockey shirt. I couldn't remember what 'ironic' meant. Nguyen spent time with the English dictionary when he wasn't reading chess books.

Mrs. Larkin was just coming out of her door when we met her. She did a double take when she saw Nguyen's sweater and said, "Did your aunt knit that?"

Boy, she could probably tell the future!

"Well never mind, you'll pass muster."

"Mustard?" said Nguyen.

"MUSTER, boy, muster. It means inspection. Bless the child, he does have his problems with the English language."

Nguyen seemed a bit shaken; I felt sorry for him. After all it must be difficult enough learning American without having New Zealandish as well—I never heard the word "muster" either. I didn't let on though.

We went up the stairs trying to look casual. There were a few people in the sightseer car, only the tiny overhead lights were on. Clouds prevented the moon or stars from shining through. No one paid any attention to us.

It was colder than ever between the sightseer and the dining car.

"No way to heat these vestibules," muttered Mrs. Larkin.

"Vestibule?" asked Nguyen.

"This space here is a vestibule," she replied. "It's impossible to insulate or heat them completely. And the baggage car won't be any better," she added grimly.

I put all thoughts of Dad out of my mind. One thing was for sure, he wasn't going to hear about this from me!

The door to the dining car slid back. Inside it was

totally dark so Mrs. Larkin's flashlight was really needed. We had to go through three cars after that, and they were pretty full. Most people had their seats tilted back and were fast asleep. The railroad supplied pillows and blankets just like an airline.

Mrs. Larkin hid her flashlight inside her purse while we walked through these cars, but once through the far door she took it out again and led the way over the metal floor to the baggage car door. It slid open, but there was no welcoming warm air from inside. Even in a hockey shirt and jeans I felt frozen.

"The baggage is stored downstairs," said Mrs. Larkin. "They don't sell tickets for the upper level unless there's a crush."

"Why is it so cold?" I asked.

"No point in heating baggage. And it discourages nosy people like us."

It was weird making our way down the aisle in total darkness except for the flashlight. Several times I bumped into seats, though I was positive I was walking dead straight.

Nguyen brought up the rear. He could just about see in the dark. I had a tougher time. Once I thought Mrs. Larkin was well ahead of me, so I speeded up and banged into her; she jumped with fright and dropped the flashlight. Of course it went out.

"Perfect, just perfect," she said in a loud whisper. "Well done, Jeff."

"I thought you were getting ahead of me," I answered miserably.

"How could I get ahead of you when we're all walking at the same pace?"

"How did I know we were walking? . . ."

The flashlight came on. "Found torch," said Nguyen. "Nothing broken. By the way, why you whisper in empty car?"

"In situations fraught with danger one always whispers," replied Mrs. Larkin in a loud whisper.

After that I let Nguyen go second; I didn't want to be bumping into Mrs. Larkin while going downstairs.

The flashlight picked out a chain at the top of the stairs. Hanging from it was a sign saying "No Admittance." Mrs. Larkin unhooked it, and we went through. Then she stopped and took a Coke from her purse, shining the flashlight on it.

"We don't want to be surprised," she explained. "I'll put this on the center of the second step. If anyone comes . . . Used it in my book *Bodies in the Belfry*."

She fiddled with the tab. "And I just let a little air in too."

We made our way down carefully. The stairs and walls were not carpeted so we made a fair bit of noise even in sneakers. Once I nearly tripped. Jeez! I was more scared of making Mrs. Larkin mad than I was of breaking my neck.

When we got down she shone her light around the

car. It was huge, like a square cave. Instead of rooms, the whole area was open except for the stairs in the middle. Suitcases, packing crates, ski equipment and sacks were dumped every which way. There was even a double bass case sticking up in the middle of a mountain of sacks. It had to be about eight feet to the ceiling.

The baggage car was real cold; the floor wasn't carpeted. The cold came up through my sneakers, just touching something metal felt like being burned.

"Where's the trunk?" said Mrs. Larkin. Her breath was white in the beam of the flashlight. "Anyone see it?"

I hadn't figured it would take much time to find a trunk in a railroad car. I was wrong. For one thing, we couldn't see anything without the flashlight so we had only one pair of eyes instead of three. Another thing was that some stuff was piled on top of other things, and so anything behind was hidden and beyond the stairs there was an equal amount of luggage.

It was Nguyen who saw it first. Mrs. Larkin had organized us when she decided the trunk wasn't visible from the steps.

"Spread out," she said, "Jeff, you watch the right, Nguyen the left. Try to go straight, and when the light's in front of you look carefully." She moved it across the car in a sweeping movement.

We'd gone about twenty feet when Nguyen shouted. "Here it is."

Mrs. Larkin and I joined him. It was the trunk, all right. I recognized it right away. It was just a couple of feet from the back wall of the car.

"You're sure?" Mrs. Larkin asked.

"Positive," I said.

Mrs. Larkin shone the light on the front of it. There was a central lock with a keyhole and a clasp at each end of the lid.

"It pretty secure," said Nguyen.

We cleared a space in front of the trunk, moving the double bass case and a dozen sacks marked "US Mail." "So what now?" I asked. "It's locked."

"Obviously," said Mrs. Larkin. "I thought of that. Hold the light."

I just managed to grab it as the light swung crazily from side to side. "Shine it on my purse, Jeff."

She dug around inside and took out a large pocket knife. "Now aim it at the center lock."

It was black; "Strongbolt Co." was painted on in little white letters. Mrs. Larkin opened the knife and pulled down a blade shaped like a little screwdriver. She grunted, and the blade scraped in the lock. At last, there was a snapping sound.

"OK boys. Stand back."

Mrs. Larkin lifted back the lock, reached down and unfastened the clasps at each end of the trunk. Then she raised the lid slowly and pushed it back until it was supported by two chains from the inside.

I shone the light inside as Mrs. Larkin peered into the trunk. She gave a gasp of surprise. "Boys, will you look at that! If it isn't right out of *The Affair of the Missing Trunk!*"

I stared past her shoulder. The trunk was empty. Not a thing in it.

"You write a book about an empty trunk?" asked Nguyen.

"The boy's priceless," she said. "I've got to put him in a book. Nguyen, boy, how can you write a book about an empty trunk?"

The flashlight wavered in my hand; there was a creaking sound. Mrs. Larkin had sat on a hamper.

There was a long silence. Then Nguyen said carefully. "No one send an empty trunk on a train."

The hamper creaked. Mrs. Larkin had got to her feet. "Go on boy. Run with it."

"Trunk not empty when it come aboard."

"How? . . ." I began.

"Because if it had been empty, Jeff, porter would have known. Might have asked awkward questions. He wouldn't forget when asked by the police. Something in trunk."

He was right. "The porter was really straining too," I said. "I remember that."

"The boy's got the bit between his teeth," said Mrs. Larkin. "I'll bet you something else too—if you tried to find the address on that label, you'd be out of luck. Jeff,

58

shine the flashlight inside. Give it a good going over."

I examined the inside carefully. It was lined in white cloth. Mrs. Larkin also looked in. "Now you're concentrating at last," she said excitedly.

I saw a brown stain in the corner. "There's a blood-stain in one corner," I said excitedly. "A real dark bloodstain."

Mrs. Larkin peered at it closely while I held the light. "That, Jeff, is a waterspot."

"Oh."

Nguyen was feeling in the far corner of the trunk, searching for something between the folds of the lining. I held the light directly on his hand.

"Saw something bright," he said. "It glimpted."

"Glinted, boy. What is it?"

"Piece of gold," Nguyen replied, holding it between two fingers.

"Gold cuff link," Mrs. Larkin said, examining it. "Cuff link all right."

"Cuff link?" said Nguyen.

"Bless the boy." She snorted. "It's a way to fasten a shirt cuff—the kind that doesn't have buttons. There's only part of it here though."

"It got letters on it," Nguyen said. "On top."

Mrs. Larkin peered at it real close. "You're right. Hold the torch, er, flashlight, steady, Jeff. I see . . . S.J.K."

Outside, the diesel horn sounded low and mournful. "We'll soon be in Devil's Lake," she muttered. "We'd better get a move on."

The Empire Builder began slowing down. We crossed a set of tracks, the wheels rattled loudly below us. The car swung first to one side then the other.

Then several things happened at once. I lost my footing and dropped the flashlight which bounced twice then went out. From the stairs came a loud shout of surprise followed by a bumping sound, an explosion, and a hiss.

Nguyen grabbed my arm. "Jeff, I dropped gold thing," he said, "it fell on floor."

This was sure to have sent Mrs. Larkin into a real spaz, but she didn't get a chance. The train was pulling into a station and slowing down. At the same time, we heard someone banging around at the top of the stairs.

"Quick," hissed Mrs. Larkin, "hide or we're as good as dead."

7

$=\!=\!0\!=\!0\!=\!=\!=\!=\!0\!=\!0\!=\!=$

"Three Pipe Problem"

IT SOUNDED TO ME IF WE MADE ENOUGH RACKET TO wake the dead. Maybe we did, but the noise from the exploding Coke can and the shout of surprise from the stairs concealed our movements from whoever was coming down. Another thing—as I moved away from the trunk, I touched the flashlight with my right hand, and picked it up.

There was a lot of cursing from the foot of the stairs. Then a powerful flashlight went on. The beam wavered across the luggage car, missing me by inches.

The only hiding place I could see, in the instant the light passed me, was between the trunk and the rear of the car. I squirmed into the space and sat facing the trunk, knees drawn up, the flashlight still in my right hand.

Behind me, I could feel the rear wall of the luggage car. It was ice cold through my clothes. I moved away because I'd read somewhere that if you touch metal that is very cold, skin will stick to it. I didn't want to find out if it was true. So I edged closer to the trunk, my nose almost touching it. I dragged two mail bags around me and tried to burrow under them.

The train was slowing down noticeably. The trunk rocked gently, then began to slide slowly towards the stairway. One of the mail sacks fell on top of me.

The only thing that saved us was that whoever was on the stairs also realized the train was stopping. The light on the stairs wobbled again and pointed up the stairs. That was all I saw. I had my own problems. I was almost lying on my side with a mail sack and a couple of skis on top of me. The point of a ski pole was jabbing in my ribs.

When I had wriggled free of the ski poles and mail bags, there was just enough time to get back behind the trunk before the train came to a halt. Outside I heard voices, and the door of the car opened. The flashlight on the stairs went off.

Someone entered the car. All I could hear was heavy breathing and cursing, followed by the sound of several heavy things being dropped on the floor. The door closed.

Within a minute the Empire Builder started up, moving slowly out of the station.

Slowly, step by step, a dark figure descended the stairs. A beam of light swept slowly back and forth across the baggage car. It paused twice, once on the double bass and once on a couple of skis sticking up almost to the ceiling. Then it vanished.

I was going to stand up, but at that instant I saw several flickers in the distance. The mysterious figure had not left the baggage car. He was in the other section beyond the stairs. When he shone the flashlight most of the time he was hidden by the stairs.

Very carefully, I got to my feet and stretched. My left leg had gone to sleep and when I tried to stand on it, I almost fell over. Then pins and needles started running up and down it. There was a crick in my neck and I had to rub it to prevent myself from crying out in pain. Jeez!

I thought I heard some moving around. No one dared to call to others, but I was sure I heard Mrs. Larkin groan softly.

Suddenly the light shot across the baggage car. I dropped to the floor, just grazing the edge of the trunk with my forehead. I bit my lip to avoid crying out. Boy, would I have a bump there. How was I going to explain that to Dad?

I was behind the trunk but wasn't hidden otherwise. I pulled one of the mail sacks toward me, but the train had picked up speed and the mailbag seemed to have a life of its own, gently edging away from me.

When I tugged at it part of it seemed snagged on the metal floor. The only light was brief flashes when the light on the stairs reflected off the walls or roof of the car.

I gave the mail bag one good pull; it fell and there was a loud crack. It's chord had been caught around one of the skis which toppled over, hitting the trunk as it fell.

"What was that?"

I recognized the voice right off. It was Nicholas Drake.

The light moved around from side to side, then settled on the trunk, lighting up the wall behind me. I could feel my heart pounding and knew he could hear it above the noise of the wheels. The light stayed on the trunk forever. Then I heard him say. "Damn skis." The voice seemed to be right above my head. Then there was the sound of something hitting the side of the car. He'd thrown the ski out of the way.

My back, which had been aching, now felt on fire. Mr. Drake was shifting things around, apparently trying to get to the trunk. Then there was the sound of metal scraping metal. "Damn key," I heard him say. "Why won't it turn?"

I was sure holding my breath now. If Mrs. Larkin's knife had broken the lock, I didn't want to think what would happen.

The key finally turned; the clasps were snapped

back. I felt the motion of the lid being raised and pushed back. It touched the sack above me and forced it down on my head.

I started to count up to a hundred by twos. Anything to take my mind off the pain in my back and the fact that I was hiding only two feet from Nicholas Drake.

He was grunting and doing something to the trunk, I couldn't tell what. I got to eighty when I felt the trunk lid close. The light in the baggage car dwindled to nothing. At one hundred sixty, I could stand it no longer. I straightened up like a released spring. One of the mail sacks started to slide off my head. Grabbing for it, I knocked a ski over. It fell on several more and they collapsed like a row of noisy dominoes.

When that was over, it got very quiet. Finally I dared to look around, the luggage car was dark, and in the distance I saw the beam of the flashlight disappearing around the top of the stairs.

Leaning forward on the trunk for support, I turned the flashlight on, catching Mrs. Larkin in the beam. She had straw sticking out of her hair.

"That was a very close call," she said. "That ski barely missed me. Now where's Nguyen?"

"Here," said my brother very faintly.

I swung the beam around. Then I saw his head sticking out of a pile of ski poles. "Thrown ski just miss me too."

Mrs. Larkin found a packing case and sat on it. "I presume that was the charming Mr. Nicholas Drake."

"Yes," I said. "Wonder what he took?"

"He not take anything," said Nguyen. "I see it all. He put something in. I not see what."

"Something in," I said. "Why?"

"Well if we open it up we won't have to guess," said Mrs. Larkin reaching into her purse and taking out the penknife.

"Knife really mess up lock," cautioned Nguyen, but she ignored him. There was the familiar scraping sound. The lock snapped open. "Come on. Lift the clasps. Jeff, focus the light."

We lifted the lid. We gazed in amazement. "This very strange," muttered Nguyen at last. "Not get it at all."

The trunk was no longer empty! Neatly arranged inside were several pairs of shorts, a pair of pajamas and a robe, half a dozen wrinkled shirts, a heavy steel picture frame, a three piece suit on a hanger built into the trunk, a dozen thick books and a heavy overcoat.

Mrs. Larkin took a long look, shook her head, then slammed the lid shut, and wrestled with the lock. Finally it clicked shut. "We'd better get back, boys," she said. "This looks like a three pipe problem."

"You smoke a pipe?" asked Nguyen, as we crossed the baggage car towards the stairs. "Not see any women in America who smoke pipes."

There was a long sigh. "No, of course I don't smoke a pipe. Surely you've heard of Sherlock Holmes? Whenever he had a difficult problem he'd smoke three pipes of tobacco, play his violin, then he'd have the answer." She started up the stairs with me behind shining the light ahead of us. "It's just a figure of speech."

"You play the violin?"

"Oh, forget it, boy. Let's get back to your room."

No one noticed us. In the dining car, the waiters had everything set out for breakfast. Mrs. Larkin sailed through.

Back in the room, Nguyen climbed into the upper berth. Mrs. Larkin went to her room and came back with a folding stool and a pot for making hot water. She had little packets of coffee, sugar, and a small jar of something called "Ovaltine."

"Well," she said. "Any thoughts?"

"It sure a three pipe problem," said Nguyen from the top bunk. "And I pretty tired."

"Any other thoughts? Important ones?" She fiddled with my night-light bulb, unscrewed it, stuck in a special plug, and watched while a red light on the pot went on.

"Well? Any observations, constructive questions?"

I thought it over carefully. It was pretty risky asking Mrs. Larkin anything. You never knew which way she'd jump. Our sixth grade teacher, Mr. McGlynn, had a sign on the wall saying. "The only dumb question is the one that isn't asked." He'd never met Mrs. Larkin.

"I don't get it," I said. "I mean why would Mr. Drake put his clothes in the trunk? Wasn't he going to sleep in his pajamas?"

"And?"

"Why would anyone," I said, getting braver, "why would anyone put clothes and books in an empty trunk?"

"Good questions." I felt my face redden so I quickly glanced out the window. She lifted the lid of the pot and tested the water with her little finger. "Ouch! It's almost ready. You get the Ovaltine."

When I got it, it wasn't too bad; it had a sort of extra-milky taste, but it sure put some warmth back into my body. Mrs. Larkin added three packets of sugar to her coffee. She ferreted around for something to stir it with. She didn't find anything so she had to use a pencil.

"In *Voyage to Nowhere* and *The Last Voyage of Mrs. Mulleycuddy*, the body is brought on the ship in a steamer trunk."

"Body?" Nguyen and I shouted together. "What body?"

"There's always a body when a large trunk is brought on board and found to be empty a few hours later," she said firmly, sipping her coffee and peering at us over the top of her granny glasses.

I was pretty sure Mrs. Larkin thought the whole world and everything in it was part of some novel. She got mad because we'd never read any of the books. I'll bet she hadn't read my dad's book on Emperor Titus.

"What I can't fathom," she said, "is how you saw them both."

"We did," I said.

"Both of them? Together?"

"Sure."

Nguyen leaned over the edge of the top bunk. "Not together, Jeff."

"Well, we heard them talking."

Mrs. Larkin gazed into her cup of coffee. "But you did see them together just before Mr. Kurtz jumped."

"We heard them arguing," I said. "Right next to the stairs."

"So all we've got is this great half empty trunk and a gold cufflink. Be sure you don't lose it," said Mrs. Larkin.

Nguyen didn't say a word; I didn't either.

Mrs. Larkin stood up, folded her stool and propped it against the wall. "Time to sleep. Meet me in the dining car at eight-thirty. Set your alarm or tell Mr. Lomax. Rugby soon. Geographical center of the United States."

She collected up her pot and the extension cord. "Perhaps the little gray cells will come up with something then."

"Little gray cells?" asked Nguyen.

"Brain cells, boy, brain cells. Will you never learn the English language?" She banged out of the door leaving Nguyen staring at her as if she was mad. Jeez! Maybe she was. How can you tell with adults?

8

French Toast

MY ALARM WENT OFF A FEW MINUTES EARLY; THERE were cloths and towels in our rooms so we decided to take a shower. I figured it would help keep me awake. We folded our bed clothes and placed them on top of the upper bunk. Once the seats were back in position there was a lot more room. The little shower worked OK, but the water wasn't very hot. I guess it was being used to heat the train. Still, it took us over thirty minutes to get ready.

"Mrs. Larkin be very impatient," said Nguyen, as we hurried through the sightseer car.

But we were in luck; Mrs. Larkin wasn't in the dining car. We ordered hot chocolate and waited.

It was almost nine-thirty before she showed up. I

was just about to start filling in my order slip when she sat down at the table.

Mrs. Larkin looked around. The waiter was already filling her coffee cup. "Notice how much more relaxed people are on the second day of a train trip," she said. "That's another reason I never travel by air. It's over too quickly. I once had to travel on the Concord. That was an experience."

She sipped her coffee, made a face and poured in more sugar.

"It a mighty fast plane," said Nguyen, drinking his chocolate.

"Dreadful meals," snorted Mrs. Larkin. "You can balance a ten pence on its edge, but the filet mignon is like leather." Picking up the menu she added, "Now what have we here?"

I'd already read it and thought it was pretty good. There were eggs, juice, coffee, ham, bacon or sausage, and toast. All for three fifty.

Mrs. Larkin was filling in her slip rapidly. Nguyen and I had to hurry because the waiter was standing over us. When we'd done, he took all three slips, carefully putting Mrs. Larkin's on top. I'll bet the cook got to work on that one first.

"I ordered French toast for all of us," she said, "because it's very good on this route." Sipping her coffee she glanced out of the window. "And the Western omelette for myself; it's safe enough as long as they don't use a microwave oven. Have you ever had an egg from a microwave? Disgusting!"

The train began slowing down; my chocolate slopped up and down inside the cup.

"Minot," said Mrs. Larkin. "Coldest place on earth. Crew changes here. Spent a night here once. Freezing hotel room. Pitiful restaurants. I was on a book tour. You boys wouldn't know what a book tour is, I suppose?" She turned to us. My eyes were fixed on the table; Nguyen was looking into his cup.

"Hrumph! Thought not. It's something cooked up by publishers. You get booked in at one horse towns," she stared at Nguyen as if challenging him to ask what a one horse town was. He didn't. "Then," she continued, "you talk on some fifty watt radio station to six people."

She sat back and took a long drink of her coffee. "Now I did get on Johnny Carson once. That was the night a giant goliath beetle flew in his face. Wonderful moment. He went over backwards and half the audience scattered for the exits. They make a noise like a soccer rattle. The man who brought it said he didn't know it could fly. Ha!"

We didn't ask what a soccer rattle was.

I glanced out of the window. A freight yard with some car barns behind it slid by. We crossed switches and pulled into a small station painted white. Long icicles hung from the roof. A porter was dragging a cart

73

with several cardboard boxes on it along the platform. His breath was one long white stream.

A group of men in Air Force uniforms was assembling on the platform. I saw the black man who had helped Mr. Lomax. A porter with an electric baggage cart drew up to them, and they threw the luggage on to it, slapping their hands together to keep them from freezing. One of them threw a snowball at another. In seconds a snowball fight erupted. Then they left by the exit. I could see a small bus outside the station.

Because the train was late, we were moving almost immediately. The waiter placed three glasses of juice on the table. Almost immediately the little paper mats under them were stained orange.

Outside the land was flat and snow-covered. Here and there were level irregularly shaped spaces that must have been frozen ponds.

"Nothing," commented Mrs. Larkin "for miles upon wasted miles except missile bases and oil wells."

She was right. Everywhere almost nothing except the snow moved. Here and there were oil pumps rocking up and down.

The French toast arrived. Mrs. Larkin also got what the waiter called her morning "pick-me-up." It looked like tomato juice. Jeez, I hate tomato juice. The French toast was great; there were three different kinds of syrup.

Mrs. Larkin's omelette was okay. She told everyone in the dining car, and the waiter looked mighty relieved.

"That your favorite breakfast?" asked Nguyen, after a while.

"No boy. It isn't. You can't beat kippers and fried bread aboard the Flying Scotsman."

Nguyen was smart, he didn't say anything after that.

I could tell Mrs. Larkin was thinking. She ate in silence. Finally, when we'd finished and the table was cleared, she sat sipping coffee and looking out of the window.

"It's got me foxed, boys. I just can't put the pieces together."

"The little gray cells didn't work?" asked Nguyen.

She ignored that. "Why would anyone creep around in the middle of the night in a freezing baggage car just to fill a trunk with clothes, a picture frame, and some old books?"

"Wrinkled clothes at that," I added.

She nodded and poured the last of her coffee from the pot to her cup. The waiter took it away before she'd had a chance to ask for more.

"Wrinkled," she muttered. "Why wrinkled?"

"Come out of small suitcase," Nguyen suggested. "All squashed up."

She looked at him, then out of the window, then back at him. "Right," she said loudly. "Right!"

The couple at the next table looked up in surprise.

Mrs. Larkin got to her feet, searching through her purse, and threw three five dollar bills on the table. Then she hurried down the car, almost knocking down the waiter who was bringing a fresh pot of coffee.

Back in our room, she took one seat, we took the other.

"Nguyen hit it," she said excitedly. "Always said the lad had promise." She slapped his knee, and I think he blushed.

"Someone put clothes in that trunk because they didn't want any questions if it were ever opened. There was a good chance it wouldn't be until the railway gave up trying to deliver it to the phony address. Then when it was opened, they might think there's a lot of wasted space, but it doesn't raise the questions it would if it were completely empty."

She drummed her fingers on the ledge by the window. "What I can't figure is what the trunk was for." She leaned forward. "At first, I must confess that I thought Mr. Kurtz's body was in it."

"That would explain the cuff link," I said, "but he was alive when the train left Chicago."

It was snowing again. Vast drifts had blown up against the utility poles along the track. There were places where the snow was higher than our window. We seemed to be sliding through tunnels of snow and ice.

"Look how high the snow is," I said.

Mrs. Larkin, who had been looking out of the window, stopped drumming with her fingers and peered sharply at me.

"Wait a minute, wait a minute. Say that again Jeff," she said.

"I just said 'look how high the snow is.' "

"I'm losing my touch," she said, getting to her feet. "Who was taller, Mr. Kurtz or Mr. Drake?"

"Mr. Drake," I said.

"Mr. Kurtz," answered Nguyen, at the same time.

Boy, I thought Mrs. Larkin would go through the roof at that. Instead, she grinned like a Cheshire cat.

"Get it?" she demanded.

I turned to Nguyen. "Mr. Drake was a bit taller. When they came on board . . ."

"But Jeff," Nguyen interrupted, "they didn't come together." He put his hand on my arm. "We never saw them together."

"No," said Mrs. Larkin with a note of triumph in her voice. "You never saw them together." She slid into her seat and held each of us by the arm. "Because they never were together."

"But they talk," said Nguyen, "we hear that."

"And how did Mr. Kurtz talk?"

"He sounded a bit hoarse," I said.

"And is that the way he normally talks?"

Boy, was that a dumb question. "How should I

77

know," I said. "I never heard . . ." My voice trailed away. "I never heard him speak before."

Nguyen spoke slowly, as if afraid of making a mistake. "We never hear Mr. Kurtz speak before. Voice could be anybody's. Could be . . ."

"Mr. Drake's," I finished.

"See it all now," said Nguyen, his eyes fixed on Mrs. Larkin's face.

"Well, boy, let's have it."

"Mr. Kurtz come on board. We see Mr. Kurtz, but not much, he pretty hidden by hat and scarf and big coat. Could be anybody."

Mrs. Larkin's eyes were shining. She was loving every minute of it.

"Maybe he do quick change. . . . rush out, board train again"

"Yes? Yes?" Mrs. Larkin nodded rapidly.

"Later, there a loud quarrel. Hear two voices, see no one until we find Mr. Drake leaning out of door. He say Mr. Kurtz jump, but no one see him."

I felt shivers down my spine. Before he told me the rest of it, I'd figured it out and I said, "Because Mr. Kurtz was already dead. His body was in the trunk. Mr. Drake went to the baggage car, took it out of the trunk, opened the door, and threw the body out knowing it might never be found or, if it was, too long after the murder to prove anything. Then he made a big scene for our benefit."

"And Mr. Drake took the money," Mrs. Larkin finished. "That's for sure."

"I'll get Mr. Lomax," I said, beginning to get out of my seat.

"No you won't," Mrs. Larkin said, pushing me firmly back. "There's not a scrap of proof, and anyway this is our show. We'll prove Mr. Drake's a cold-blooded killer. And we'll do it this very night in the baggage car." She paused. "This very night, boys."

And she sat back positively licking her lips. Jeez!

9

Mrs. Larkin Has a Chat

THING WAS WHEN MRS. LARKIN TOLD US WE WERE going, I got nervous. Dad would have died before he'd have let us go into a freezing baggage car at night on a train in the middle of nowhere. Mrs. Larkin didn't bat an eye. Nguyen was looking at me as if waiting for a lead.

"Perhaps we should tell Mr. Lomax or the conductor," I ventured again.

"Hrumph," Mrs. Larkin replied. I took that for a "No".

"What we have to do next, boys, is to beat the covers." She stared at us. "Now if you don't understand a term don't be afraid to ask. I'm always willing to explain things. The only stupid question is the one you don't ask." Nguyen and I looked at each other, and he winked and mouthed, "Mr. McGlynn."

"To 'beat the covers' means we have to scare up a bird or two. Now we've only got one bird, and I want him edgy. Nervous men make mistakes, possibly let the cat out of the bag.

"I want you boys to find Mr. Nicholas Drake and keep your eyes on him. I shall take a little snooze and brew up some coffee around eleven."

Off she went, humming.

"Why she make coffee?" asked Nguyen when she was safely out of the room. "You can get free coffee any time."

"Well she's pretty old," I said. "She must be over fifty. Old people get these habits, and they stick to them forever."

Nguyen and I had to find Mr. Drake. We went to his room first and listened. There wasn't any sound. Then we made our way up the train to the sightseer car, but he wasn't there either. We waited while the train began to sway from side to side as it crossed other tracks. A line of freight cars slid past the window. Most of them had "Conrail" painted on the side. The Empire Builder slowed to a halt.

"Willeston. This is Willeston," said the conductor over the intercom. "Mountain Time, please set your watches back one hour."

No one got up to leave, but I did see several people

fumbling with their watches. Nguyen's watch was a digital, and I would have needed a book to find out how to alter it. Mine just wound backwards when you pulled the stem out.

We sat down while the train was in the station. There didn't seem much point in moving until everyone settled down. Mr. Drake wasn't going anywhere, that was for sure. He'd have to go through with it or else. Any sudden change of plan would sure look suspicious.

The Empire Builder jerked back and forth as it pulled out of the station and built up speed.

"Look," said Nguyen, pointing out of the window.

A small herd of antelope was bounding alongside the train, clearing snowdrifts effortlessly.

"They can reach sixty miles an hour," said one of the attendants who was walking by. "I've seen them pass the train."

Willeston vanished behind us in seconds. The track became smooth and straight, the swaying motion almost disappeared. We went back down the car. Everyone seemed to be fiddling with watches and small alarm clocks. Two Japanese were standing and talking to an attendant, but he couldn't understand them.

Nguyen said something to them, and suddenly they were all smiling and bowing.

"What was that all about?" I said, as we moved on.

"Not understand about turning watches back one hour. Japan all same time zone."

We found Mr. Drake in the Amcafe car. He was sitting at a little table with a can of beer and a hamburger on a paper plate. He'd had only one bite of the sandwich and pushed it to one side. He was staring out of the window at the steadily falling snow.

Nguyen went back for Mrs. Larkin while I waited by the water fountain. In a few minutes Nguyen and Mrs. Larkin returned. She had on one of those smock dresses that button up the front.

With Nguyen and me trailing behind, she sailed down the car until she reached Mr. Drake's table where she pretended to be surprised to see him.

"How do you do?" she said, sticking out her hand. "I'm Agnes Larkin. We didn't have time for a formal introduction this morning."

Mr. Drake got slowly to his feet and took her hand hesitantly. "I'm Nicholas Drake."

"This is Jeff and his brother Nguyen," added Mrs. Larkin, taking the seat next to Mr. Drake and motioning us to sit opposite. She pulled her purse up on to the table and began searching through it. Finally she found a pack of cigarettes and took one out.

"Do you have a match?" she asked.

Mr. Drake put down his beer and felt in his jacket pocket. He produced a box of matches and gave it to her.

"I was very sorry to hear about Mr. Kurtz," she said, striking a match and lighting the cigarette. The box had "Players Navy Cut" on the side. Mrs. Larkin blew out smoke in a long stream.

Mr. Drake coughed and waved his hand in front of his face to get rid of the smoke. He looked embarrassed. He wanted to get up and leave, but Mrs. Larkin had him cornered.

"It was a terrible loss," he said.

"Was he a good man to work for?"

"Oh yes, yes," he nodded. "A very fine man. But, of course, he had become very unstable these last few days."

"Stress," said Mrs. Larkin. "It creates havoc with the system. I'm a writer so I ought to know." She paused and stared fiercely at him. "A well-known writer of mysteries." She drew herself up to her full height. "I won an Edgar with *Death Comes in Threes.* You have heard of it?"

Mr. Drake shifted in his seat. "Well I may . . ."

"They don't give Edgars away in cereal boxes. It sold over two hundred thousand copies, but I suppose that only gives me a chance of one in . . . one in . . ."

"A thousand," said Nguyen. Mrs. Larkin leaned in close to Mr. Drake and said confidentially, "He's a very smart boy, English is a bit weak, but then how good is our Vietnamese, eh?"

At this she dug her elbow in his ribs and laughed.

That was enough for Mr. Drake; he started to get up. "It was a pleasure," he said, "but if you'll excuse me, I have to get back to my room. It's been a very tiring day, as you can imagine."

"Of course, of course," Mrs. Larkin said soothingly, but not moving an inch. "I suppose you've heard the latest." She looked around as if she expected to be overheard.

Mr. Drake sat down again. Mrs. Larkin knocked ash from her cigarette into the tin ashtray.

"Heard what?" he muttered.

"The attendant said there was a small gold cuff link found in the vestibule. Not all of one, just a part, you know."

Mr. Drake took a long drink of beer as he considered that. "So what?" he said finally.

"Why, I'll tell you what," said Mrs. Larkin, motioning him forward so their heads were almost touching. "I heard Mr. Lomax say that the F.B.I. would be searching the train at Portland to see if they could find the rest of it. To trace Mr. Kurtz's movements, don't you see?"

Boy I'll say this for Mr. Drake; he didn't panic. I would have. He moved back in his seat and gently twirled his beer can between his fingers, all the time looking at our reflections in the window.

"Mr. Kurtz was with me," he said, at last. "All the time."

"Oh, of course, of course," said Mrs. Larkin crushing out her cigarette. "There's no suggestion of foul play."

"Foul play!" exclaimed Mr. Drake loudly.

"Shush," Mrs. Larkin patted him on the arm. "You know what the F.B.I. is like. They probably will ask a few questions, search the cars, get statements. Just to prove they're on the ball."

At the second mention of the F.B.I. Mr. Drake began to look a bit scared. His voice wasn't so firm when he spoke. "But why the F.B.I.?"

"The accident did take place during interstate travel."

I thought he seemed a bit paler too. Mrs. Larkin picked up on this.

"There now I've upset you," she said, sounding real concerned. "I'll leave you to your sorrow." She stood up. "I suppose they will go through my suitcases and the trunk I have in the baggage car. Oh, it's really too much."

She was gone almost before we knew it. We followed. Back in our room, Mrs. Larkin plugged in her hot water pot. "Well we've put a little ginger in our fox," she said with satisfaction.

"But won't he go straight to the baggage car right away?" I asked.

Mrs. Larkin sat down on the seat opposite still looking very pleased with herself. "Not if I know the criminal mind, he won't. For one thing, he can't be sure where the rest of that cuff link might be. He will search his room first. There will be no one to bother him there. If he finds it, he knows he's safe since Mr. Kurtz could have broken it any time.

"All the time, the baggage car and the trunk will be on his mind. Finally the penny will drop. The only possible place left will be the trunk."

"And he'll wait until night to go to the baggage car," said Nguyen. "No one there to bug him; Mr. Lomax not around either."

Mrs. Larkin's pot was boiling. She got up, turned it off, and began carefully measuring spoonfuls of Ovaltine into three Styrofoam cups.

"Yes. Remember I told him the F.B.I. wouldn't be on board until we reach Portland. So he knows he has tonight all to himself. No one will disturb him."

Mrs. Larkin added water to each cup. "Tonight we'll be in the baggage car when Mr. Nicholas Drake comes hunting for the evidence. Then we'll know he's guilty."

She pointed a finger at each of us. "This isn't like a book boys, this is for real. Dress warmly!"

10

The Baggage Car

THE WAITING WAS THE WORST PART OF IT. THE EMPIRE
Builder, already an hour late, was falling further and
further behind schedule as we began the long climb to
the Rockies. Passengers were already bugging Mr.
Lomax about what time we'd be in Portland. He had a
place at the end of one of the forward cars, just beyond
the dining car, he called an office. It was two seats
facing each other where he kept a briefcase, the schedule, and several walkie-talkies. Once when he came up
the train, Nguyen asked him what the walkie-talkies
were for. He could talk to the engineer and the Central
Dispatcher with it. It was powerful enough to be picked
up sixty miles away.

The snow was no longer falling and the air was
clear. Above, the sky was deep blue. We were definitely

climbing now, and around curves the cars sloped in slightly. At a town called Glasgow, we followed a frozen river for miles; it had to be a river because even though it was covered with snow and frozen, it was the only flat area for miles. Here and there the track had a solid rock wall on one side and a steep drop off on the other. But the Rockies were still ahead and only when the train followed a curve did we see the peaks rising straight into the sky.

Mrs. Larkin had gone to her room after lunch saying she would have a nap before our adventure. Jeez, I knew I couldn't sleep.

Nguyen was sitting on one of the seats with the chess set on the little table. I was looking out of the window.

"Wonder what Jenny Weber is doing now," he said suddenly.

I turned to look at him. "Jenny?"

He nodded. "She probably working on some experiment."

"Or bugging Miss Boswell at the library." I laughed. Jenny was the girl who'd helped us nail the art smugglers at Loon Lake. She wanted to be a scientist and was forever talking about becoming a doctor or something.

"Or borrowing somebody's ten speed," added Nguyen.

He was lucky, he had a Huffy dirt bike; Jenny liked my ten speed.

"Wonder if we'll ever see her again," I said.

"If we go to the cabin we will," replied Nguyen.

For a long time we didn't say anything. The countryside rolled along beside the track and every so often an antelope leaped up from nowhere or a snow rabbit hopped over the snow.

"Wonder if I ever see my parents?" Nguyen muttered. It was so quiet, I could barely hear him.

That was the first time I ever heard Nguyen say anything about his folks. He'd been airlifted to an orphanage in Japan; that was where Mom found him. She'd told us the Red Cross was making inquiries. That was five years ago and he'd been in the orphanage for five years before that. I didn't know what to say, so I just stared out of the window. Pretty soon out came Bobby Fischer's book and Nguyen started to play chess.

After a while I left our room and wandered up and down the train aimlessly. Mrs. Larkin was right about train travel. Passengers were chatting away as if they'd known each other for years.

I don't know how I got through the afternoon. One thing's for sure, there was no sign of Mr. Drake. A "Do Not Disturb" sign was hanging from the door knob of Bedroom E. I'll bet he had gone over every inch of his room looking for the bit of the gold cuff link.

The announcer made the early dinner call, and Nguyen came looking for me a few minutes later.

"Mrs. Larkin say we go to dinner car right away," he said. "She finished nap and raring to go."

"Raring to go?" I asked.

"She say that. It not English?"

"Must be New Zealandish," I answered.

Mrs. Larkin had already ordered for all of us. The maitre d' showed us to the table we'd had before. There were fresh yellow flowers in a big vase. Everyone else had a small rose in a thin vase. She didn't even look up when we took our seats. One waiter was pouring her a glass of pink wine and another looking at her order slip and making rapid pencil notes. I was surprised to see two glasses of Coke on the table.

"The prime rib, can't risk anything else—medium rare, of course," she was saying, "baked potato, sour cream with chives, tossed salads, vinegar and oil dressing for the boys, Russian for me."

She tasted the wine and nodded. The other waiter looked mighty happy and refilled her glass.

"Soon be at Havre," Mrs. Larkin said to us. "Twenty-five minute stop, crew change. If you look out of the windows over there you'll see the Bear Paw Mountains on the horizon. It's beginning to get dark too."

I caught myself shivering. I couldn't help it, but I drank a little Coke hoping no one would notice.

The Empire Builder was almost two hours late as we pulled into Havre. Nguyen and Mrs. Larkin were eating their steaks as if nothing was wrong. We were about to get into a pitch black luggage car with someone who probably killed his boss, and all Mrs. Larkin could do was complain that there weren't enough chives in the sour cream and comment on the scenery like a tour guide. Jeez!

A few people got off the train to stretch their legs, but they didn't stay long. There was a huge steam loco behind a chain link fence. Mrs. Larkin pointed at it with her steak knife. "Nothing as romantic as a steam engine," she declared. "Metal wheels on iron rails, the hiss of steam in the cylinders."

Nguyen looked at me; his mouth formed the word "Dad."

Mrs. Larkin didn't notice. She put her knife down and took a sip of wine. "My father, God rest his soul, took me on the Evening Star on his last visit to England. It was loco 92220 if I remember."

"As big as that one?" I asked.

"Not that powerful; it was a 2-10-0 but the driving wheels were small to give it traction at low speeds. It was intended for freight originally, but it hauled passenger trains at eighty miles per hour. Papa was very sick, but he wanted one last ride so we booked tickets from London to Manchester. That was in 1964. A year later he was dead and the Evening Star was replaced by a diesel." She wasn't talking to anyone in particular, and when she stopped Mrs. Larkin carefully laid her knife and fork together across her plate leaving her meal unfinished.

The waiter took her plate away.

There was a sudden blast of icy air. An attendant had opened the vestibule door and was trying to clear away the snow. It was so cold with the door open, he gave up. The train pulled out almost immediately.

Mrs. Larkin didn't seem to be in too much of a hurry. She drank three cups of coffee using an artificial sweetener from her purse. She stared longingly at her pack of cigarettes but didn't light one. Nguyen and I had chocolate; it was red hot and a welcome change from Ovaltine.

When she was ready, Mrs. Larkin took up the bill and paid it. She always paid, and I didn't know if we were supposed to offer to pay our part. I just couldn't bring myself to ask either. On TV the man always pays. He reaches into his pocket and scatters bills on the table and everybody's happy. Suppose he didn't pay enough? Sometimes he's with a lady, and she walks out; then he throws the money on the table, but he hasn't seen the bill. Most of the time he's ordered, and no one says what they do with the food that's left over. I once . . .

"Jeff!"

I looked at Mrs. Larkin; she was standing up, Nguyen by her side.

"What?"

"I said 'let's go to the sightseer car because we're coming to the Continental Divide.' What on earth were you thinking about?"

"Nothing," I muttered. Again I felt myself blushing. Nguyen was grinning. Mrs. Larkin shook her head.

The sightseer car was right next to the diner, but it was weird getting to it. The Empire Builder was going up the mountainside, but we were walking downhill. Outside, the sky was a bright gold color, and the snow seemed sort of red instead of white. All the lights had been turned off so everyone in the car looked bronzed.

We found a seat; Mrs. Larkin took it while we stood on each side of her.

We weren't going very fast; there was an announcement that we were following a freight train and couldn't go any faster than it was traveling. The car was filling with people because it was the last night of the journey, and by breakfast the trip would be over for most of us. They wanted something to remember, and they soon got it.

As we approached Glacier National Park the scenery was so great that I forgot about Mr. Drake for a while. Everyone was "oohing" and "ahhing" as a solid wall of mountains appeared to the north. On the right side of the train there was a sheer wall of rock, with icicles hanging down like huge daggers. On the other side were drop-offs and deep valleys filled with evergreens covered with a white blanket. Every so often the snow got too heavy and a tree bent so far the snow fell off. Then the evergreen popped up like a green jack-in-the-box and everybody cheered. We went through snow sheds—tunnels built with wood so that an avalanche would pass right over us, and several times saw mountain goats looking down at us curiously from ledges along the mountainside.

Finally we reached Marias Pass; Mr. Lomax came on the speaker and told us we had crossed the Continental Divide. Everyone applauded and some people opened bottles of champagne.

"What if Mr. Drake goes to the baggage car now?" I whispered to Mrs. Larkin.

She shook her head. "He won't do anything until we reach Libby," she said confidently. "Then he's got two hours of uninterrupted time to search."

And so we sat and waited. Mrs. Larkin was offered a glass of champagne, and she sat looking out of the window, sipping away as if nothing was going to happen.

We were well over two hours late when we reached Libby. We set our watches back an hour, but no one could figure out if that made us three hours late or one. Nguyen said it made no difference. If anyone would know, he would.

Mrs. Larkin was fiddling with a silver pocket watch. "This time change business has possibilities for detective stories. Think how significant it was in

Around the World in Eighty Days." She glared at us. "I don't suppose you read it?" We shook our heads.

"I saw the movie," I said. Mrs. Larkin sniffed in disgust. "I don't know what they do in schools anymore. I suppose it's Dungeons and Dragons and video arcades these days."

No one got on or off at Libby, but through the gloom we saw Blue Mountain towering over the town.

Mrs. Larkin put her watch away in her purse. "All right. Give me ten minutes, then I'll join you in your room. It's going to be very, very cold. So put on everything you've got. Especially gloves and under-shirts. Two pairs of socks, don't forget." And off she went.

I hate undershirts, but I put on two of them and a sweater under my Oilers shirt.

"That Mrs. Larkin crazy, for sure," said Nguyen. "If Dad ever find out about this we lobster meat." He tugged his sweater over his head.

"Crab meat," I said automatically, but he didn't hear.

We both looked like rag bags when we'd finished. Nguyen not only had his shoes on, he'd pulled on a pair of socks over them. He also had on his parka, a ski cap and fur-lined gloves. Since Dad had done the packing, there were some things missing. There wasn't an extra pair of socks in my case, so Nguyen had to give me the pair he had on over his shoes.

Mrs. Larkin knocked on the door. She had a thick blue overcoat and the buttons were straining. There was a scarf over her head and a pair of leather gloves on her hands. She also carried a blanket.

"I'd like to see this fellow hoist with his own petard," she said.

"Me too," agreed Nguyen.

She glared at him sharply, but he looked her in the eyes without blinking.

"The big problem will be getting through the sightseer car," she went on still glaring at Nguyen, "looking like tramps. You'll have to take off the more obvious things—ski caps and gloves—and put them in your pockets. Each of you will need a blanket so get them."

When we reassembled she added, "We go one at a time and just walk naturally," she ordered. "Jeff go first, Nguyen last."

She was right of course. The sightseer car was still pretty full and we did get a few stares. The diner was ready for breakfast, not a soul in it. And the three cars beyond were half full and almost everyone had the seats back and the leg rests out. No one paid much attention. Mr. Lomax wasn't in his office as we went by. We were just like people about to settle down with a blanket for the night. Anyway, the lights were all dimmed down.

At the end of the car, we just kept on going. There

wasn't anybody there because it was much colder near the unheated baggage car.

The vestibule was so cold I felt my sneakers sliding on ice that had formed on the metal. My teeth started chattering. Mrs. Larkin's flashlight went on. I heard her muttering to herself; then the light shone on her hand. There were two sticks of Juicy Fruit gum.

"Chew these. It will stop your teeth chattering, boys."

The steps down to the baggage compartment were in the middle of the car. That meant I had to inch my way along, keeping my hands stretched out in front of me. Mrs. Larkin decided to go first with the flashlight, which didn't help Nguyen or me much. We tried to walk straight, aiming ourselves at the flickering light.

The car seemed endless but finally I felt the side of the stairwell. A blast of cold air from the baggage area below hit me. As we edged down the stairs, it got colder. Much colder than I remembered from our last visit. Now we were up in the mountains for one thing; for another, the car had been out in freezing weather for one more day.

"The best thing to do is to use the blankets and baggage as insulation," said Mrs. Larkin. "Wriggle underneath some of the bags, but put your blanket around you first."

"Suppose he not come?" asked Nguyen. "It very cold."

"He'll come, boy. Have no fear. Oh and take these." There were more rustling sounds. The light shone on two Milky Way bars. "They'll give you energy," she added.

She aimed the light around the car so we could find somewhere to hide. For once I got lucky. A big packing case had a loose piece of wood; when I reached inside and pulled a whole pile of straw came out. That, the blanket, and a couple of mail sacks made a place to hide.

"Don't sit on the floor," Mrs. Larkin said. "It will make your body freeze faster if you do."

I pushed a bunch of straw under me. Already I felt better.

"Everybody settled?" she hissed.

"Yes," Nguyen and I answered together.

I stared at my watch. Exactly midnight. Jeez!

11

Musical Chairs

SITTING THERE I BECAME CONSCIOUS OF EVERY SOUND,
even though the wheels under us were much louder
than in the other cars. Still, whenever Nguyen or Mrs.
Larkin moved, I heard it plainly. Worse, now that the
excitement was beginning to wear off, I got cold
quickly. There was no way to keep warm even with the
blanket and straw. I couldn't get comfortable either. By
twelve thirty, I was paralyzed. Clenching my hands, I
took off the gloves and blew on my fingers. I tried draw-
ing my hands up inside my sleeves. Nothing helped. My
toes were worse. Taking off my shoes and rubbing the
toes only helped for a few minutes. As soon as I put my
sneakers back on, the cold crept back through my body.

I remembered the candy bar and took it out for a
minute just to savor it. When I tore the paper, the

sound seemed deafening. I bit a piece and let it dissolve slowly in my mouth. I made it last as long as possible. It was great, but it didn't warm me.

I kept looking at my watch. The luminous dial showed up all right, but the hands didn't seem to move. At least it was ticking. I thought about Nguyen. He couldn't see his digital without pushing a button. I wondered if the light would give him away.

Soon it was so cold I thought I'd freeze stiff. I remembered Mr. McGlynn saying that you couldn't die by falling asleep in freezing weather because after a while you'd be so uncomfortable you'd wake up. I didn't believe it.

Suddenly I began to shake; I was scared, real scared. I wanted to get up and run back up the stairs, through the short icy vestibule, back into the warm cars beyond. I might have done it, too, except that at that exact moment a beam of light cut through the darkness from the top of the stairs, wobbled, and came to rest on the steamer trunk.

Someone was standing on the top step; I couldn't see more than a faint dark shadow behind the light. But I knew who it was all right.

The light crossed the car and came to rest on the stairs, then jerkily the beam seemed to descend, the dark shadow following close behind, until finally both paused at the foot of the steps. Then the beam of light crisscrossed the car—trunks, skis, boxes, and packing cases were briefly illuminated then disappeared into the darkness.

Now I could hear the sound of someone making his way across the car. The beam of the flashlight was aimed down in front as he checked his way across the floor. It wavered once or twice as the train swayed.

The flashlight stopped on the trunk. There was the sound of a key being fitted into a lock and some muttered curses. A loud click followed. Soon after, the two clasps snapped back.

The light bobbed around, occasionally vanishing as it was aimed deep into the trunk. There were more muttering sounds.

There was a loud thumping noise. Now the trunk was lying on its side, lid flat on the floor. Mr. Drake was kneeling on the lid and feeling with his hands along the folds of the trunk lining. He had wedged the flashlight between two suitcases so he had both hands free.

"Is this what you're looking for," Mrs. Larkin's voice came out of the darkness. I couldn't see her and neither could Mr. Drake. With a snarl, he scrambled out of the trunk, grabbed the flashlight and shone it around wildly. He didn't see anyone.

"It's over here," I said.

The flashlight spun around. The light passed right across my hiding place. Jeez!

"Here," called Nguyen, getting the idea fast.

I hadn't figured on what Mr. Drake would do next;

he played it real cool. Instead of waving the light around, he suddenly turned it off. There was a lot of banging and cursing. Then nothing.

Mr. Drake didn't know where we were, but we didn't know where he was either. And so we waited. Boy, was it unnerving. I could hear nothing but the rumble of wheels on the rails. I sure couldn't see a thing.

I put myself in Mr. Drake's place. What would he do? He wouldn't stay in the middle of the baggage car. The thing to do was to get back to the steps. That way no one could get past him and go for help.

He wouldn't stay at the bottom of the stairwell either. It was cold enough on the steps but a lot warmer than it was on the metal floor where we were crouching.

Sure enough when the flashlight went on again, it was almost at the top of the stairs.

"Well, well," he said, carefully playing the flashlight across the car. "One old busybody and two nosy kids. You just had to interfere, didn't you? Couldn't leave well enough alone."

"You killed Mr. Kurtz, didn't you?" said Mrs. Larkin.

The flashlight whizzed across the car and caught Mrs. Larkin in its beam. She was standing behind a wire cage. I stood up too. Red hot needles shot up my legs; every muscle was on fire, and I was scared my legs wouldn't work. The light settled on me.

"So. Where's the third blind mouse?"

Nguyen didn't say anything, but I heard him moving to my left. The light darted across the car. He was half hidden behind a packing case. Only his head and shoulders showed.

"Yes. I killed him. He found out I'd been stealing the money so I killed him and put the body in the trunk. Then I threw it off the train so it would look like suicide. Anything more you want to know?"

I got a real sick feeling, and it wasn't just because Mr. Drake had confessed. I wondered why he was telling us all this stuff. I soon figured it out. He was going to see to it that we never told anyone.

"And you pretended to be two people, didn't you?" continued Mrs. Larkin.

"And it would have worked if you hadn't stuck your beak in where it wasn't wanted. Now I shall have to arrange a little accident. You'll freeze to death in here."

"Boys," said Mrs. Larkin. "When I say the word, hide in a different place.

"What's this?" snapped Drake.

"Now," said Mrs. Larkin.

The flashlight moved wildly around. I lay behind a long thick roll of carpet with skis piled on top.

"Musical chairs won't help," shouted Drake. "You've got to pass me to get out.

Mrs. Larkin was smart. She figured he'd never

come after one of us because the other two could escape and get help; we were moving around and keeping warm, and there wasn't anything Mr. Drake could do about it.

"Move again, boys."

I crawled behind a large crate.

The flashlight went out. There was a long silence. No one spoke, then I heard the sound of metal against metal. The door of the baggage car rumbled open. A blast of ice-cold wind howled in through the opening, blowing light snow everywhere. I shuddered, and it wasn't just from the cold.

"Feel that?" shouted Mr. Drake from the safety of the stairs. "Feel that ice and snow. When they check this baggage car in a couple of hours, you'll be frozen stiff. It's two hours before the next stop. Maybe longer. By then you'll be all iced up." He gave an evil laugh.

"You'll never get away with another murder," shouted Mrs. Larkin.

The flashlight stayed off. He didn't care where we were. There was only the sound of the wind howling outside and the dim outline of the sheer cliff walls outside.

"No murder," shouted Mr. Drake. "Just an unfortunate accident. And don't think you can close those doors. Things get icy and jammed up in this climate. Maybe the three of you could do it. I'd like you to try."

"He push us all out," said Nguyen loudly.

"Right," shouted Mr. Drake. "But why bother? I've done the impossible—a perfect murder. Soon I'll have four . . .Hey, what's this? . . ." He broke off, surrounded by flashlights.

Seconds later, the door slid shut. Above us lights went on in the ceiling of the car. On the stairs stood the conductor, Mr. Lomax, and half a dozen attendants in Amtrak uniforms. Two of them were holding Mr. Drake. He soon gave up struggling, and stood there glaring at us.

"I'm glad he didn't know about those lights," said Mrs. Larkin, stretching her arms and stamping her feet.

"You need a key," said the conductor, showing it.

Mr. Drake shrugged his shoulders. "You can't prove anything. I know the law. I'm a respectable businessman and that counts for more than the opinion of a dotty old woman and two sniveling brats." He stopped, then added triumphantly. "By the way, I discovered a little gold something by the trunk. It's somewhere in the Rockies if you want to look." Then he laughed loudly.

The Amtrak attendants were puzzled. Mrs. Larkin turned to Nguyen. For once she didn't blow her stack. She shook her head sadly. "He's right boys. That cuff link was our only piece of material evidence. Now it's our word against his."

I felt sort of sick inside, mostly for Nguyen.

"Not just our word," said my brother moving towards a large packing case with "Electrical Parts" stenciled on it in white. "Told lots of people."

"The boy's crazy," said Mr. Drake. "I deny everything."

From the top of the packing case near the stairs, Nguyen picked up a small object.

"Borrow Mr. Lomax walkie-talkie," he said holding it up. "From top of mountain words probably reach hundred fifty miles. Mr. Drake hoist with his own petard."

Mr. Drake gave a scream of rage and almost broke free. It was several minutes before four men wrestled him to his knees. There he stayed, his head down, chest heaving.

Mrs. Larkin turned to the attendants and said proudly, "This boy will be magnificent." She added to Mr. Lomax in a much quieter voice. "Of course, he'll have to work on his English a bit first." Then she looked down at Mr. Drake. "This is just like the end of one of my mysteries," she added with satisfaction. "Justice triumphs!"

What Mr. Drake said can't go in a book.

12

Lobster Meat

WE HAD A LOT OF EXPLAINING TO DO. THE EMPIRE
Builder made an unscheduled stop at Bonner's Ferry,
and the sheriff took Mr. Drake off to jail.

Mrs. Larkin told us she would tell Dad everything,
but Mr. Lomax told her that was the conductor's job. I
was glad. Dad wasn't going to be too pleased when he
heard what happened. He was sure trains were safe and
nothing could happen on them. He'd be very disap-
pointed, especially as Nguyen and I both had gotten
bangs on our heads.

We almost didn't make it to breakfast. I was so
tired I fell asleep before Mr. Lomax made up the bottom bunk. He had to wake me up. I let Nguyen take the
top one again—I didn't think I could climb up.

It was eight o'clock when Mrs. Larkin banged on

our door. "Meet me in the dining car in thirty minutes. Pack first."

When we got to the dining car, there was no sign of Mrs. Larkin. The waiter handed us a note.

"Boys," it read, "I can't stand goodbyes. I'm sure you understand. I've talked to the F.B.I., you'll find them very understanding. Look for a book based on our little escapade."

> *Your friend in crime,*
> *Agnes Larkin*

Secretly I was kind of glad. I hate goodbyes myself and though Mrs. Larkin didn't look like the kissy-kissy type you could never tell. Worse still, I just knew Dad wasn't going to be thrilled by her explanations.

When the train finally pulled into Portland, Nguyen and I were in no hurry to get off. I told him to be sure to wear a hat over the Band-Aid. I covered my bump too. When it couldn't be delayed any longer, we got down slowly with our suitcases. Mr. Lomax said he'd join us in a couple of minutes.

It was cold on the platform, but there was no sign of snow anywhere. I soon caught sight of Dad. He was walking along anxiously, looking in all the doors. The Seattle cars were being pulled away at the end of the platform.

Rodney was trailing behind Dad, eating a candy bar; he had on his new glasses—the ones with the aviator frames. Dad let out a whoop when he saw us. "Hi guys," he said, running up and hugging us both. "Great to see you. Your Mom's at a rehearsal now. We'll see her at lunch. Good trip?"

"Well, Dad . . ." I began.

"I envy you," he went on. "Trains are such fun. The clickety-click of the metal wheels on the iron way. Give me your impedimenta."

Dad taught at a university and was always using strange words. I wasn't going to ask him what a petard was, though.

He struggled with our suitcases while looking for a cart; there wasn't one of course. "We'll have to carry our own," he said. "Rodders and I had a very dull flight. Which was just fine."

"It's like this Dad . . ." I started.

"But do you know what I like about trains?" he went on, interrupting me. "You can put boys like you on a train and have two days of peace and tranquility knowing nothing is going to happen. Right, Rodders?"

"Right, Dad," said Rodney.

Out of the corner of my eye, I caught sight of the conductor, Mr. Lomax, and two other men in dark business suits moving towards us.

I put my suitcase down and took a deep breath. There was no escape. "The fact is, Dad, there was some trouble on the train. We've got to stop and have a talk with the F.B.I."

Dad stopped so suddenly that Rodney bumped into him and dropped his candy bar.

"The F.B.I.?" Dad asked, faintly. "The real F.B.I.?"

Right then I knew if we were only grounded for a month, we'd be real lucky.

Rodney even forgot about his candy bar.